More praise for *Roadkill*

"Friedman writes breezily about Indian medicine bundles and a villain called the Green Arrow, but his real passion is having his alter ego—fueled as always by cigars, espresso, and copious amounts of Jameson's Irish whisky—indulge in as many wisecracks, riffs, puns, asides, and rude one-liners as possible."

—*The New York Times*

"Author Richard Friedman was given the nickname Kinky for his curly 'Jewish natural' hairdo, not for his sexual proclivities. But it might just as well have been for his writing style, which is full of twists and turns and Friedman's particular brand of skewed humor. All of which are displayed in his latest mystery novel, *Roadkill*."

—*USA Today*

"He endures as one of the few intentionally funny writers in a rapidly filling dance card of mystery writers. . . . The internal voyage is what's important in this book. I've compared Friedman to Jack Kerouac in the past; this book is like *On the Road* meets *On the Road Again*. Friedman's work is always laced with witty turns of phrase. . . . My favorite line from all of Friedman's work comes in this book: 'Imagination, of course, is the money of childhood.' "

—*Houston Chronicle*

"With *Roadkill*, Friedman cinches his credential as a great Southern storyteller. He combi⸻⸻ ⸻ ⸻ductive moxie of a Chandler or a Hammett wit⸻

of a stream-of-consciousness raconteur, and the blend is a pungent delight."

—*Fort Worth Star-Telegram*

"Like all truly off-center artists, Friedman is one of a kind, a gifted writer. . . . Kinky is rapidly becoming an authentic American institution, a latter-day Mark Twain."

—*The Knoxville News-Sentinel*

"The tenth mystery, starring Kinky as Kinky, is his best in years, largely due to the guest-star appearance of singer Willie Nelson. . . . Kinky's kvetching mope is an excellent counterpoint to Willie's Zen Texan. Let's hope we see them paired again."

—*Booklist*

ROAD

KILL ⚠

KINKY FRIEDMAN

BALLANTINE BOOKS • New York

A Ballantine Book
Published by The Ballantine Publishing Group

http://www.randomhouse.com

Library of Congress Catalog Card Number: 98-96298

ISBN: 0-345-41632-5

This edition published by arrangement with Simon & Schuster, Inc.

Cover illustration by Marvin Mattelson
Cover design by Janet Perr

Manufactured in the United States of America

First Ballantine Books Edition: September 1998
10 9 8 7 6 5 4

To Roger Friedman, the first manager of the Texas Jew-boys, who came to Nashville for three days to help his brother and stayed for three years.

> "And I'd ride the Silver Eagle to the
>   last town on the line
> Railroad ties are not, my friend, the
>   only ties that bind. . . ."
>
> from "The Silver Eagle Express"
> by KINKY FRIEDMAN and
> ROGER FRIEDMAN 1973 BMI

Three fingers whiskey pleasures the drinkers
Movin' does more than the drinkin' for me
Willy he tells me that doers and thinkers
Say movin's the closest thing to bein' free

Willy you're wild as a Texas blue norther
Ready-rolled from the same makin's as me
And I reckon we'll ramble till hell freezes over
Willy the Wandering Gypsy and Me

—Willy the Wandering Gypsy and Me
By BILLY JOE SHAVER

CONTENTS

PART ONE

HELL

"When you're going through hell, keep going."

—WINSTON CHURCHILL

CHAPTER ONE

YOU COULD SAY the whole adventure began the day I looked in the bathroom mirror and saw the gypsy. That explanation might not hold up in a court of law, but as far as I'm concerned it's close enough for country dancing. I'd come in rather late the night before and as I slept I was visited by a strange and singularly vivid dream. Without going into graphic details, let me just say that I finally came across the girl in the peach-colored dress who was being held captive by a remote tribe deep in the jungles of Borneo. By disguising myself as a middle-aged orangutan, I was at last able to secure her release but not, however, before they took two Frisbees and used them to make her lips big.

By the time I woke up it was already late in the afternoon. Hell, I thought, if I'd been a banker I'd have been through for the day. Of course, if I'd been a banker I probably wouldn't have been living in a cold, drafty loft with a little black puppet head sitting wistfully on top of the refrigerator with the key to the building wedged in its mouth. If I'd been a banker I wouldn't wake up to garbage trucks grumbling bitterly outside my window. Or a lesbian dance class pounding away on the ceiling above. Or a cat performing tai-chi exercises upon my sleeping scrotum. On the positive side of the ledger, of course, was the fact that if I'd been a banker I probably wouldn't have been able to remember my dreams.

I leaped sideways out of bed, put on my purple Robert Louis Stevenson bathrobe, went into the kitchen, and located a wayward can of Southern Gourmet Dinner. As I opened the can, I glanced down at Vandam Street through the frost and the grime on the kitchen window. It was not clear precisely how much of this mucouslike obfuscation was on the outside or how much was on the inside of the window. As far as the outside went, you could probably blame most of the crap upon cars, people, pigeons, and God, none of whom have been known to be greatly concerned about the messes they've created on the outside of windows.

To be completely fair, it must be noted that incessant cigar smoking can occasionally lend a subtle, yellow-brownish, stained-glass-like appearance to the inside of windows. Whether this phenomenon manifests itself as Flemish or merely phlegmish is arguable. Beauty, as they say, is strictly in the eye of the beer holder.

I fed the cat the Southern Gourmet Dinner, opened diplomatic relations with the espresso machine, then bounded into the bathroom to go about my various morning ablutions. I climbed into the rainroom for my annual shower and as I washed the temple of my body, which, in some areas required the painstaking efforts of an archaeological dig, I began to sense a certain cleansing of the windows of my soul. It was time I got out of New York for a while, I figured.

My career as a country singer-turned-private-investigator appeared to be taking a turn for the worse. After a promising little string of successfully solved cases, for some unknown reason clients now seemed to be staying away in droves. Not only was my professional life moving along with all the fluid grace of a midtown traffic jam, but my personal life had slowed to a virtual standstill as well. My entire existence, I reflected as I washed my left armpit, was currently about as exciting as rich people watching bats.

I jumped out of the rainroom, dried myself off with a colorful towel left over from a recent Hawaiian adventure, and segued smoothly over to the dump machine, where I donned my hydrogen mask and took a prodigious Nixon which I won't go into too graphically so as not to step on Chaucer's toes. It is enough to say that when I got off the dumper I felt better about cars, people, pigeons, and God, in, of course, a random and haphazard order.

Like any other post-Nixon morning, I got back inside my purple bathrobe and walked over to the sink. Like any other post-Nixon morning, I expected to cross the miles and miles of bathroom tiles only to stare into the silver distance of the bathroom mirror at those waving fields of emptiness that had become the country of my heart. Alas, this was not to be the case.

There, staring back at me, was a countenance very similar to my own, except that it appeared to be slightly more real and substantial than I felt at the moment. The face was almost mine but the eyes seemed different. They burned with the intensity of campfire embers, remembering everything I'd thought I'd forgotten. Nor was the figure wearing my purple bathrobe; he was swathed in a flaming tunic from a long-ago era. His hair was not a Hebrew natural like my own; he wore it long and dark and shiny and all wrapped up in a bright red sash. A silver earring hung from his left ear. Not like those commonly worn today by athletes, homosexuals, and teenagers, soon, perhaps, to hang themselves while masturbating and die from autoerotic death syndrome. This gypsy had been born with his earring, and it fairly gleamed with all the stolen mischief of dreams.

I blinked my eyes several times but the image in the

bathroom mirror did not go away. They never really do. The bathroom mirror is the perfect place for you to one day see the gypsy in your soul.

"Who the fuck are you?" I said, in some dream state of mild hysteria. If you can talk to a cat, I figured, you can talk to a bathroom mirror.

"I am the gypsy in your soul," he said, "and I have come to tell you a little story that makes, I'm afraid, about as much sense as your life."

At that precise moment, I was pretty sure he was going to be right. Still I tried to preserve reality, to save sanity.

"Hold the weddin'," I said. "I don't even know your name. Do you have a card?"

"My name is Antonio," said the gypsy, "and this is my card."

Clearly in the bathroom mirror I could see him holding up the king of hearts.

"Start talkin'," I said.

"One dark, stormy night," the figure intoned, "a band of gypsies was gathered around the campfire. The leader stood up and said, Antonio tell us a tale, and Antonio stood up and said, one dark stormy night a band of gypsies was gathered round the campfire and the leader stood up and said, Antonio tell us a tale, and Antonio stood up and said, one dark stormy night a band of gypsies was gathered round the campfire—"

"I see the problem," I said. "Not only do I have a gypsy in the bathroom mirror, but he happens to be the most tedious gypsy in the world and he appears to be talking to me on an endless loop."

"Now you understand. Come away from there. Come travel the world with me. Leave your loft and your village and your friends and your cat and Stephanie DuPont—"

"How'd you know about Stephanie DuPont?"

The gypsy said nothing, but his eyes sparkled like Romanian stars.

I felt many things just then as, mesmerized, I gazed into the mirror. Fear, curiosity, disbelief, desire. When I finally spoke again it was to voice a sentiment that was not uncommon amongst many New Yorkers.

"But how can you travel so far away?" I said.

"From where?" said the gypsy.

CHAPTER TWO

IF GOD hadn't wanted us to talk to gypsies, I figured, He wouldn't have created bathroom mirrors. Of course, then nobody'd have been able to see their wrinkles and everybody'd be running around looking like biblical nerds and Hitler wouldn't have been able to trim his mustache and whores with hearts of gold wouldn't be able to touch up their makeup and death-bound teenagers wouldn't be able to pop their zits before the prom and everybody else would be going crazy brushing their left nostrils with their toothbrushes and frantically trying to find their Prozac or their heroin suppositories behind the bathroom mirror that wasn't there anymore. So I let the gypsy slip through the silver fingers of somebody else's dawn and thought about something my old friend Dr. Jim Bone had once told me: "If you get tired of looking at yourself in the mirror try looking at yourself out the window." I tried that for a while but I'd never had much of a view.

The puppet head smiled hopefully from the top of the refrigerator. Office workers headed for the subways like leaf-cutter ants along avenues of oblivion. Pigeon wings fluttered almost ethereally against the window-panes. Cockroaches scuttled silently across the sink. I sat at my desk sipping espresso and smoking my first cigar of the day like a brokenhearted Romeo who'd decided at the last minute to just keep on living, if you wanted to call it that.

It was a short while afterward, as leaden layers of dark clouds began suffocating the sky, that I noticed my hands were shaking slightly. It's not every day you carry on cocktail chatter with a gypsy in the bathroom mirror. But it wasn't just the appearance of the gypsy that was bothering me. It was the gypsy's ability to see inside my mind and my soul and then relate to me what these worn and weary vessels contained, whether or not I'd been aware of it myself. Stephanie DuPont, for instance. The gypsy must've plucked her right out of the sadness in my eyes. She wasn't even in New York. As far as I knew, she was still in Florida, ostensibly staying with her aunt and uncle whose names were Hank and Audrey, if they existed at all.

I'd come to the conclusion that Stephanie was actually hanging out down there with various spiritual riffraff in a dedicated, persistent, ruthless effort to hose McGovern and myself out of our shares of Al Capone's buried treasure. I'd flown to Florida with her a lifetime ago with the highest of hopes and returned several months ago with no treasure and no Stephanie. I hadn't heard from her in all that time, but now, as I walked to the window, I saw a chauffeured limousine snootily slither up Vandam Street. I watched the driver, who had his own key and didn't need the puppet head, open the doors of the building and emerge minutes later carrying Stephanie's two little dogs, Pyramus and Thisbe, who'd been entrusted to Winnie Katz, the lesbian line-dance leader from the loft above. I watched from the window as the little dogs yapped their way out of my life, and the limo rolled inexorably past a phalanx of garbage trucks and out of sight. Then I went upstairs and knocked on Winnie Katz's forbidden door.

"Come in," she shouted.

I turned the knob, opened the door, and entered the secret sanctum of the sisters of Sappho with the mild trepidation that any man would feel.

"Fuck," she said when she saw me. "I knew I should've locked the door."

"Despise no man," I said in a conciliatory tone, "and call no thing useless."

" 'Thing' is a polite word for it," she said.

Winnie was sitting at her kitchen table with her hair back in a rather severe ponytail, and was wearing an extremely well-fitting pair of hot pink leotards. She looked pretty good if you didn't know better. She was drinking her usual Red Zinger herbal tea and smoking a cigarette from a pack with a skull and crossbones emblazoned on it.

"Try a Death Lite," she said, pushing the pack toward me. "I get them from London."

"Still on a health kick, are you?" I said, as I took a Death Lite and lit it up. My hand, unfortunately, was not as steady as I might have wished.

"You don't look so good, Sherlock," she said. "You look like you've just seen a ghost. Or did the departure of Pyramus and Thisbe finally break your little heart?"

The fact that you've just seen a gypsy in the bathroom mirror is not something you particularly want to share with any passing lesbian. But my relationship with Winnie was a little different and, in fact, at one time, had almost been one.

"Maybe you just need to get away from the city for a while," she said, not unkindly. I couldn't help but notice the look of pity that had crept into her eyes.

"This summer I'm going back to Texas," I said.

"You'll never make it," said Winnie. "It's only November."

So we sat at that little kitchen table in New York smoking Death Lite cigarettes with darkness closing in all around us and I told Winnie about the gypsy. She sipped her Red Zinger herbal tea and seemed to take it all in understandingly.

"Let me get this straight," she said, "for want of a better term. You saw a gypsy in the bathroom mirror and you asked him for his card?"

"It was kind of a joke."

"So are a lot of things in life," she said, as she gazed out the dark window. "Then he holds up a playing card? A king of hearts?"

"Yes, Dr. Freud."

"Then the gypsy tells you to come roam the world with him and you ask how you can travel so far away and he says, 'From where?' "

"That's what he said."

"Smart fucking gypsy."

I chain-bummed another Death Lite. I waited while Winnie went over to the stove and poured herself another Red Zinger. I'd passed on a cup for myself. You've got to draw the line somewhere with people or else you'll cease to exist.

I watched the Death Lite smoke circling around my head and thought of lofts and lesbians and little dogs and gypsies. Hitler hadn't liked gypsies or homosexuals much. Killed millions of them along with six million Jews give or take a few hundred thousand. He lived in a bunker. Didn't go for lofts much. He liked dogs all right though.

"You know," Winnie was saying, "she's not coming back."

"I know."

"I miss her, too."

"I know."

"But I miss her in ways that you don't know."

"I know."

"You probably ought to see a shrink. I would, if I'd just spent half the afternoon talking to a gypsy in the bathroom mirror."

"I know."

"But you won't do that?"

"No," I said. "But I like your frog umbrella stand."

Winnie got up from the table and stood by the window. I waited and watched her back, which wasn't a bad view for a New York apartment.

"You can't stay," she said. "I've got a new group coming in and you'd only make the girls uncomfortable. In fact, you're making me uncomfortable."

"I know."

"You don't know *shit*," she said, spinning around to face me and looking very desirable in her righteous anger. "Stephanie's gone. The little dogs are gone. Your mind is gone. Your eyes make you look like either Rasputin or Richard Nixon, I can't decide which. And you won't go to a shrink. There's only one other thing you can do."

"What?" I said, as I killed my Death Lite.

"Go with the gypsy," she said.

CHAPTER THREE

THAT'S EXACTLY what I did, of course, though I probably didn't realize it at the time. I thought I was merely going through some kind of midlife crisis that required me to drink large quantities of Jameson Irish Whiskey from my old bull's-horn shot glass, watch cobwebs form on the little Negro puppet head, and feel desperately sorry for myself as only a former country singer can. I'd obviously missed my chance to become a teen suicide. Now all that was left for me was a ragged, weary, cynical world with all the spiritual ambience of a karaoke bar in Dallas.

These were my thoughts two days later as I sat drinking at my desk, trying to determine what the hell was causing a ringing sensation in both my ears. If you hear a ringing in your left ear it means, in this right-handed world, that people are saying bad things about you. If you hear a ringing in your right ear, it means people are saying nice things about you and, given the perversity of human nature, you are very likely dead. If you hear a simultaneous ringing in both ears you have a serious problem. It means people are ambivalent about you. They can't decide whether or not to invite you to join them at the karaoke bar.

On this day, though, it only took a numbed-out nanosecond or two for me to realize that the ringing in my ears was not of a spiritual origin. It had merely been caused by the two red telephones on either side of my desk ringing

at the same time. This was not surprising, because, as per
my instructions, they were connected to the same line. At
the time they'd been installed it seemed like a pretty good
career move. Made the office look important. Made the
calls sound important. You just had to remember not to
lay your head down on the middle of the desk.

"Start talkin'," I said, as I hoisted the blower on the
right.

"It's a potty!" screamed an exuberant, familiar, ro-
dentlike voice.

It was Ratso.

Ratso was my erstwhile Dr. Watson, who'd helped me
on a number of my early investigations before he'd either
inherited or not inherited 157 million dollars depending
on what the lawyers said each week. I was still waiting for
the money Ratso owed me and I probably would be for
the rest of my life.

"It's a potty!!!" he shouted again, this time a trifle
louder, if that were possible.

"Yes it is," I said. "With whom do you wish to speak?"

But by this time Ratso was entirely unmindful of any
protestations I might've made. He was caught up in a
rather puerile, near-hysterical chant, only some of which I
was able to understand. It sounded like this: "There's
going to be a potty! A very love-ly pot-ty! I'm invited to a
pot-ty! You're invited to a pot-ty! We're going to a pot-ty!"

If you have any doubts that a white adult Jewish-
American New York male could carry on in this fashion,
you've never met Ratso. And you're probably better off
that way, for what adds tedium to his character is not
merely the fashion in which he carries on, but also the
hideous fashions he inevitably wears.

"Ratso," I said, "I'm begging you to stop."

But Ratso did not stop. And though he was always
one for a "potty" as he called it, his almost insane enthusi-

asm for this particular function, I must report, had piqued my curiosity.

"Where's the party, Ratso?" I said, in spite of myself.

"It's top secret, Kinkstah," he said. "Can't tell you till you get there."

"Which is never going to happen."

"I will tell you this," said Ratso, sensing that I was nibbling at the hook. "It's a very upscale, extremely lavish, surprise-going-away-party with lots of food, a full free bar, and gorgeous broads."

"Christ," I said, winking at the cat, "how'd we get invited?"

"Can't tell you that. You knew the guy a long time ago but he's been out of touch for a while. He's a big admirer of yours, though. But he's very paranoid. When you meet him you'll understand why I can't tell you more."

"When's the party?" I said, rather halfheartedly. Not that I was the hottest party favorite in town, but Ratso had used me on any number of occasions to worm his way into places he never could've crawled into without me by his side.

"Didn't I tell you?" said Ratso. "The party's tonight."

I looked around the dusty, drafty loft. The cat followed my gaze. Neither of us saw a thing. Only a half-empty bottle of Jameson stood out on the counter to break up the skyline of loneliness. I had to admit there was room on my dance card.

"You still there, Kinkstah?"

"In a manner of speaking."

"Cheer up, Kinkstah! I'll come by and get you and we'll go to the potty together. Just like old times."

"I warn you, Rat, if I don't like this guy or this party—"

"You'll be home in a flash."

"Okay."

"I'll pick you up at eight, Kinkstah."

I hung up the blower and I looked at the cat. She seemed to be shaking her head, but it might've just been my nerves. I walked over to the Jameson, poured a healthy jolt into the bull's horn, and poured it down my neck. Then I turned and looked again at the cat. She now seemed to be gazing at me with that look of mild, hopeless dismay that all cats occasionally give to all people.

"Don't worry," I said. "If I run into a handsome young prince with a serious shoe fetish, I'll leave the party at once."

CHAPTER FOUR

AS THINGS turned out, the evening did afford a number of surprises. The first was that Ratso was punctual and pleasant, though he did appear to be dressed like some turn-of-the-century gay matador.

"Kinkstah!" he shouted from the frozen sidewalk. "Forget the puppet head. Come on down. We'll be late."

"Okay, Yorick," I said, to the puppet head, which smiled stoically from its perch. "You can take the night off."

The cat, who did not like Ratso in the first place, stared down from the windowsill at his ridiculous outfit with that look of extreme disgust cats keep in stock for only very special occasions.

"Just be glad he's not coming up," I said.

The cat, of course, said nothing, but did appear to be somewhat relieved.

I put on my black thousand-miler tuxedo jacket, which had once belonged to the actor Dean Stockwell, grabbed a handful of cigars from inside the porcelain head of Sherlock Holmes, put on my cowboy hat, and headed for the door.

I left the cat in charge.

I took the freight elevator with the one exposed lightbulb down to the drab little lobby, where some kid had left his tricycle. New York is really no place for a kid to grow up. If you're a kid you should try to grow up somewhere else if possible. If you have to grow up in New York, at least you'll grow up quickly, and before you know it, like adults everywhere else, you'll wonder why you bothered.

"Ratso," I said, once I'd joined him on the sidewalk, "you didn't tell me this was a costume party."

"It's not," said Ratso.

"Well, that's a nice outfit anyway, but where's your coonskin cap?"

"At the dry cleaner."

"Sorry to hear that. Hope they don't use too much starch. A lot of good coonskin caps get ruined that way. Of course, very few have the actual face of the coon sewed to the front of the cap."

"Follow me, Kinkstah!" shouted Ratso, blithely ignoring my attempt at pre–cocktail party chatter and heading at rapid pace up Vandam toward Hudson.

"How do we get there? Flying on your cape?"

"You'll think you are," said Ratso, as he stopped in the middle of the sidewalk and gestured rather expansively across the street. "There she is."

Parked in the midst of a small armada of garbage trucks was a long, sleek vehicle that jarred my not-so-distant memory. It was a baby blue Rolls-Royce complete with uniformed Aryan driver. Indeed, he was already standing on the curbside holding the door for Ratso and myself.

"Don't tell me this is the same car Donald Goodman used to own," I said as I followed Ratso's large buttocks into the plushly upholstered backseat.

"Donald won't be needing it anymore," said Ratso.

"No," I said, admiring the interior, "I suppose he won't."

Actually, I was pretty damn certain Donald Goodman wouldn't need the car anymore. My California private investigator friend Kent Perkins had blown him away over a year ago and gone through some rather tedious trials and tribulations, I might add, because the gun he'd used wasn't properly licensed in New York. Laws, of course, were made to be broken.

"The car is not officially quite yet mine," Ratso explained, "but until the will is fully litigated, my lawyers let me use the car and driver from time to time."

"Kind of like borrowing the family DeSoto?"

"Kind of," said Ratso. "Except it's not a family and it's not a DeSoto."

If you've ever ridden with a large Jewish man wearing a red cape and matching dead man's shoes and smiling at you like the devil himself in the back of a baby blue Rolls-Royce recently borrowed from an evil, murderous cousin who currently was riding a pogo stick in hell, you can be sure it is not a spiritually uplifting experience.

But the driver drove cheerfully on through the shadowy canyons of the nighttime city. He seemed to know where he was going, which was a hell of a lot more than I could say for myself. It was at about this time that Ratso blindsided me.

"I understand the city's starting to get to you," he said, a little too casually. "I hear you might be thinking of going away for a while."

"Where'd you hear that?" I said, lighting a cigar and cracking the window a couple of inches.

Ratso looked straight ahead and continued to smile maddeningly. "Got another cigar?" he said.

I gave Ratso the cigar and myself a little time to think. Not that it was that shocking a piece of gossip, but the way Ratso was smiling it seemed almost even money that he knew more than he was letting on.

"How'd you find out, Rat?"

"About what?"

He was giggling to himself now, almost choking on
his cigar. At that moment, I wouldn't have been eager to
administer the Heimlich maneuver if he'd been choking
to death. Mouth-to-mouth would've been out of the question.

"I think you know goddamn well what I'm talking
about," I said, with some little indignation.

"You mean the gypsy in the mirror?" he said.

CHAPTER FIVE

YOU TELL a cat or a lesbian dance instructor anything these days, I thought, and you might as well tell the whole damn world. Of course, Ratso refused to tell me how he found out, on the grounds that he was protecting his sources. Irritating me even further was the way he repeatedly pronounced the word "sauces." I was stewing in my own as the driver obliviously drove the Rolls along the glittering, potholed, wayward web that is sometimes known as the streets of Manhattan.

"Are you up for the potty?" Ratso asked.

"Is Alan Dershowitz Jewish? Of course I'm up for the potty. But before we get to this wonderful potty, you're going to tell me how you knew about the gypsy."

"Big fucking deal. So you talked to a gypsy in the bathroom mirror. So he talked to you a little bit. That's happened to a lot of people. Then, of course, men usually come and take these people away to the Pilgrim State Mental Hospital—"

But I'd already stopped listening. I was busy doing a little deductive reasoning. I'd only mentioned the gypsy to two people. One of them was Winnie Katz, who knew none of the Village Irregulars and, to the best of my knowledge, didn't even know what a Ratso was. For Winnie and Ratso to have moved in the same circles was a geometric impossibility. The only other confidant I'd had in this increasingly unpleasant and mildly embarrassing

matter was the cat. And the cat, I knew for certain, de-
tested Ratso with an irrational feline fury predating that
of the tiger in *The Jungle Book*.

So how did Ratso find out about the gypsy? It did not
appear to be a deep or dark or deadly mystery, but a
mystery it was, none the less. It was more your trifling,
trivial, tedious type of mystery. The very kind, it might be
noted, that so often eventually become deep and dark and
deadly. If I were any kind of private investigator at all, I
thought, it shouldn't take me long to figure out the solution to this pathetic little puzzle. At the moment, however, I had to admit, even though we were in the middle
of Manhattan, I was fairly well out where the buses
don't run.

"Look, Ratso," I said, "I'm very tired and it's quite
possible that I may even need a little checkup from the
neck up. So, much as I'd like to go to your party, I think
I'd really rather you take me home."

Surprisingly, Ratso did not object to my entreaty.
Maybe my condition was more obvious than I'd thought.

"Driver," Ratso said, in the tired, world-weary tone of
one who's had a driver all his life, "please take Mr. Friedman and myself back to Mr. Friedman's—uh—building
on Vandam Street."

This was out of character, too, for I'd never known
Ratso to miss a party of his own volition in his entire life.
So I sat back in the comfort of the Rolls and watched the
traffic, like life itself, dully, mindlessly, inexorably, passing
me by. When we finally turned onto Vandam Street I was
feeling like anything but a party animal. A quiet evening
with the cat, the puppet head, the bottle of Jameson, the
bust of Sherlock Holmes, and a good cigar was looking
pretty good.

"You still going to the party?" I asked Ratso, as the
driver opened my door.

"Of course," said Ratso. "I told my friend I'd be there."

"I thought you said it was a surprise party."

"You don't miss a thing, do you, Sherlock?"

"Well, it was a nice ride, Ratso. Whoever your friend is, tell him I'll see him in the funny papers."

"I'll do that, Kinkstah."

I was opening the door to the building when I noticed Ratso getting out of the Rolls and preening his cape on the sidewalk.

"You don't look too good, Kinkstah," he said. "I'll just see you to the elevator."

"That won't be necessary," I said, as I stepped into the open doorway of the freight elevator and noticed Ratso following me across the tawdry little lobby.

"I'll just ride up in the elevator with you," said Ratso, a hint of a mischievous smile ticcing lightly on his lips.

"That won't be necessary," I said, as Ratso walked into the elevator and the doors closed behind him.

We rode up in silence, but it ended abruptly when we reached the fourth floor. Even before the elevator doors opened I could hear the noise and the music. Seconds later I had an unobstructed view into my loft with the door wide open revealing a crush of partygoers. Some I recognized. Some appeared to be total strangers. As I stood in the hallway, I caught a brief glimpse of Sherlock Holmes's pale blue porcelain eyes staring balefully at me through the happy throng. The cat was nowhere in sight. I turned to Ratso. He shrugged his shoulders rather theatrically and the red cape rose and fell like a giant curtain.

"Surprise!" he shouted over the din. "It's a potty!"

CHAPTER SIX

IF YOU'VE EVER been the victim of an unwanted surprise party you know that you have the right to remain silent and that anything you say or do may be used against you. The first thing I tried to do was to get the hell out of there. I pushed the button for the freight elevator, and when I realized that it would probably take the gestation period of a giant sea turtle to arrive I ankled it over to the stairwell. But I'd only taken two or three steps toward freedom when I suddenly found both of my shoulders enmeshed in an iron grip.

"Sorry to have to detain you," said a smooth, familiar voice.

It was Rambam. Rambam was a private investigator who'd spent some time in federal never-never land and was currently wanted in every state that began with an "I." He'd also been a big help to me in almost every case in which I'd been involved, the notable exception being my search for Ratso's birth mother. Rambam was not a big fan of Ratso's.

"I think you'd better stick around," he said. "The puppet head's getting drunk and we may need someone to keep it from falling off its perch."

"We may need someone to keep me from falling off my perch."

"That's what I hear," said Rambam. "That's why I agreed with Ratso that I should do a little B&E job on your loft tonight while he lured you out of it for the first time in weeks. I never agree with Ratso, as you know, but that gypsy in the mirror shit scared me a little. The only thing I'd hate worse than having to talk to Ratso is having to take you to wig city."

Ratso had gone in to the party, and now, as Rambam and I were loitering in the doorway, we could see him in his red cape flowing from person to person like lava swirling around some small Italian village that is about to become a future tourist attraction. I still did not see the cat.

"Who are all these damn people?" I said, as I lit a cigar in the hallway and dispassionately watched the mindless mechanics of people interacting with people.

"Some you know and some you don't know," said Rambam with a fairly wicked smile, "but at least it's an opportunity to make new friends. Like the interracial couple I just met hosing on your bed."

"I'm glad *somebody's* hosing on my bed," I said.

"That's the spirit," said Rambam, and we walked in to the party.

Food, drinks, and people were everywhere. Whoever'd catered the affair apparently had thought of everything, including providing a sizable number of friends I didn't have. The music and the chatter was so loud you couldn't tell if Winnie and her girls were up there or not. Possibly they were down here. Everybody else was.

"What's happenin', dude?" asked a young guy who looked like Ichabod Crane. I noticed he was drinking from my old Imus in the Morning coffee cup.

"Careful with that cup," I said.

Rambam had drifted over to a luscious-looking redhead and I found myself tangled in a torrent of talking strangers. Then a large, friendly, familiar face loomed into view.

It was McGovern. He had a big smile and he was carrying a big drink.

"Got to hand it to you, Kink," he said. "You really know how to throw a party."

"I'd like to get a forklift in here and throw all these bastards out."

"Present company excluded, I hope," said McGovern, laughing over the white noise of the party.

McGovern was truly one of my best friends in the city as well as the world. When he laughed, the world might not have laughed with him, but at least it heard him.

"I hear," said McGovern in confidential tones, "that you're seeing little green men yourself these days. That can be rather unpleasant. For one thing, nobody believes you. I know from experience. Of course, mine have gone away now."

"Just like I wish all these goddamn people would go away. And long as I live, I'll never be as crazy as you."

"A little defensive, aren't we? But then it is true. You *are* seeing something?"

"Yeah."

"What?"

"A gypsy," I said quietly.

"A gypsy?" said McGovern, with a worried expression on his face. "Then there's only one thing you can do."

"What's that?"

"Ask him if he wants a drink," said McGovern.

The party seemed to wind on interminably, but I did have to grudgingly admit it was starting to lift my spirits a little. Part of this, of course, may have been because of some of the spirits I was lifting and pouring down my neck. I'd located the cat hiding in the bedroom closet along with my old college buddy Chinga Chavin, who was probably crazier than McGovern and myself put together, which was probably what had made him one of the most successful advertising executives in the city.

"Come on in," said Chinga, motioning from the closet. "You've gotta try a little of this. If you think you're seeing a gypsy this'll catch you up to the whole caravan."

Being cross-addicted to virtually everything on the planet, I figured if I tried one thing I might as well try another, and I went into the closet. Soon I was so high I needed a stepladder to scratch my ass. The cat looked up disapprovingly.

"Too bad," said Chinga. "You just missed seeing an interracial couple hosing on your bed."

I pirouetted out of the closet and goose-stepped over to the house phone at the Hotel Friedman.

"Extension sixty-nine," I said. "Housekeeping, please."

CHAPTER SEVEN

TURN OUT the lights," I said to the cat, much later that night as I was changing the sheets on the bed. "The party's over."

The cat sat on the far corner of the bare mattress, staring at me with deep feline irritation. She thrashed her tail back and forth rather demonstrably, but said nothing. It was just as well, considering the mood I was in.

"Don't look at me so goddamn sanctimoniously," I said. "Just because I'm changing the sheets after an inter-racial couple has hosed on my bed does not mean I'm a racist. Actually, in very Gandhi-like fashion, I enjoy inter-racial couples hosing on my bed. I applaud them for their spunk, some of which I notice is still on the sheets. I applaud hunting accidents. I applaud teen suicides. I applaud the fact that most of my so-called friends think I've been busy taking Joan of Arc lessons. But I don't give a shit what they think. I'm not running for city council. In fact, I applaud the circumstances that have made it possible for me *not* to run for city council."

The cat did not look mollified by my rambling exhortations. On top of any ideological undercurrents, the cat did not like to witness people making beds. Especially when she was on the bed.

I walked out into the living room and surveyed the wreckage of the party. In a sense, I suppose, the whole thing was almost poignant. My friends Ratso, McGovern,

Rambam, Chinga, and the other Village Irregulars had
organized this rather ill-conceived event because they
were worried about my mental hygiene. Maybe they just
thought I needed a lift, but of course, I didn't. I already
had the freight elevator. Even Mick Brennan, photogra-
pher par excellence, had popped by. Joel Siegel had been
there, too, with a few kind words, presumably to get me
back on the track to oblivion like every other normal neu-
rotic nerd in New York.

Everybody means well in this world, I thought, as I
began rather desultorily straightening up the place. That's
probably why the world is in such sorry shape. Then they
all go home and you're alone again with a cat who doesn't
approve of you, a puppet head who smiles serenely down
upon the nightmare that is your life, and maybe a gypsy in
the mirror who is trying to tell you that it's time to get the
hell out of wherever the hell you are before you turn into
everything Peter Pan didn't like.

There is a time in all of our lives, I reflected, for us
to see gypsies in our mirrors. Generations of people of all
races and cultures have distrusted and persecuted gypsies
and sent them on their way to somewhere else, which, of
course, was fine with the gypsies, because somewhere else
was always where they wanted to be. The Germans gladly
would have killed as many gypsies as they did Jews, and
they tried, yet both tribes escaped extinction. God did not
let the gypsies be destroyed because he knew that sooner
or later you were going to look into the mirror and need
to see one. God refused to let the Jews be destroyed
because He knew that sooner or later someone was going
to require the services of Robert Shapiro. God did not let
the Germans be destroyed because he knew that sooner
or later Robert Shapiro would require their services to
make repairs on his BMW. Those were several good reasons, I figured, not to go to services.

"The Lord certainly works in mysterious ways," I said to the cat, who was now stretched out languorously in the rocking chair.

The cat, like the Lord, said nothing. She did not even appear to be listening. I say "she," referring to the cat. The gender of the Lord is not known to me, but as I looked around the loft and the world that night, I could safely say that whichever it was, it was likely that neither He nor She was listening. Maybe the Lord was wearing a Walkgod.

Like an unfulfilled, lonely housewife, I began clearing away the glasses and dishes and the general detritus of other people's happy experiences. I offered the cat a portion of a half-eaten pork pie that had been part of a large feast Pete Myers had apparently catered from his British gourmet shop, Myers of Keswick on Hudson Street. With a slight mew of distaste, the cat demurred. Cats realize that, of all man's many follies, the notion that there may exist such a thing as British gourmet cooking rises right to the top of the litter.

It was sometime after three o'clock in the morning when, in the fashion of a true degenerate, I lit a cigar and began sampling various drinks from glasses that people had thoughtlessly left on the counter, on the desk, on the windowsills, on the floor, and on what I sometimes liked to refer to as the furniture. Whether the glasses were half full or half empty I did not know, but drinking from them was starting to make me so high I was soon going to have to contact NASA to locate my head.

I was just working up sufficient courage to go into the dumper and check out the gypsy when the phones rang.

"Saved by the blower," I shouted to the cat.

The cat, of course, said nothing.

There's nothing wrong with periodically getting phone calls at three o'clock in the morning. It's when you stop getting them that you should get worried. It means you're either dead or you're a mature adult and there may not be as much difference between the two lifestyles as many people think. I picked up the blower on the left.

"Start talkin'," I said.

She did.

CHAPTER EIGHT

K INKY," she said. "It's Lana."

"Hey, baby. Where are you?"

"On the bus."

"Where's the bus?"

"I can't tell. It's dark outside. Somewhere in Montana or Wyoming. One of those places."

"That's rather cosmic. I was conceived in Casper, Wyoming."

"Should I call that in to the Country Music Book of Trivia?"

"As my father once told me: 'There *is* no trivia.' "

"As my daddy once told me: 'Fuck 'em if they can't take a joke.' By the way, Daddy wants to talk to you."

"He's getting fairly o-l-d to still be awake, isn't he? It's even past my bedtime."

"Daddy never sleeps."

"If you had eleven different kinds of herbs and spices in your system you wouldn't ever sleep either."

"I try. Anyway, here's Daddy."

Daddy was Willie Nelson. Willie and I had maintained a close and near-mystical friendship over the years, which had been achieved in the only manner a close and near-mystical country music friendship can truly survive. Primarily, we stayed the hell away from each other.

Lana, like Willie and almost everyone else in the Nelson family, had been married about ninety-five times, starting at the age of sixteen. Lana's most recent marriage had been to country music star Johnny Rodriguez, and the wedding, as I remember, had been a beautiful and rather poignant one, causing me to cry on two occasions. The first was when Johnny on acoustic guitar sang a soulful version of the Beatles song "In My Life" to Lana. The second time was immediately following the ceremony when Willie Nelson stepped on my foot as he was coming back down the aisle. The fact that Lana was traveling on the bus with Daddy someplace in Montana or Wyoming indicated to me that she was probably gearing up for marriage number ninety-six.

Then a familiar voice came out of the American night across the blower and the miles, in tone and timbre, I noticed, not dissimilar to the voice of the gypsy in the mirror.

"Is this Richard Kinky 'Big Dick' Friedman?" the voice said.

"Hello, Walls," I replied, a reference, for those non–country music lovers to one of Willie's first hits.

"This is Willie 'Large Scrotum' Nelson. What are you still doing in New York? Don't you know it's dangerous?"

"If I knew what I was doing here," I said, "do you think I'd still be here?"

"No, I don't. I was just getting worried you might've fallen in with that Hard Rock Cafe crowd."

The voice on the blower resonated at a spiritual frequency so close to the gypsy in the bathroom mirror it was unnerving.

"I've been thinking about you," it said.

"You haven't been projecting any auras or casting any curses, have you?"

"Why?"

"No reason. Just wondered."

"Maybe it's time we played a little chess. Maybe you

ought to get away from there. Come travel with us for a while?"

The words seemed to reverberate around my skull-house and then fall with a strange hissing sound onto my brainpan like rain in the desert I'd been blithering around in for over forty years. The words, in fact, were eerily close to the ones the gypsy had spoken.

"Come away from there. Come travel the world with me. . . ."

"But how can you travel so far away?"

"From where?" said the gypsy.

"I'm serious, Kinky, come out here and join us for a while."

"Where is here?"

"When I figure that out I'll let you know. But in the meantime, I'll let you work it out with Lana. She always knows where we are."

The texture of the sound seemed to change ever so slightly on the blower. Closer somehow. I lit a fresh cigar and waited for Willie to walk up Vandam Street, stand outside the window, and holler for me to throw him down the puppet head.

"You still there, Kinky?"

"Yeah," I said. "Did you just go into a tunnel or something?"

"No, I just went into the crapper."

I thought for a moment about the image of Willie Nelson talking to me on his cellular phone from the executive dumper on his bus. It was probably the only place in the world where Willie was ever truly alone. I'd known the feeling myself to a far lesser degree, in the distant past when I'd done some big concerts and the backstage was mobbed and the only refuge in the world seemed to be in the dumper. There was a certain irony in that, but it wasn't something I wanted to deal with at the moment.

"The dumper's kind of a special place," I said finally. "For a guy like you it must be almost your only goddamn sanctuary."

"No shit."

"Do you write songs in there?"

"Sometimes. Write songs. Meditate. Pray a lot. Most of the time I pray holding my dick."

"Very time-effective," I said. "Are you doing that now?"

"No," said Willie. "I'm just kinda starin' into the bathroom mirror."

PART TWO

TEXAS

"I'm going back to Dallas, Texas to
see if anything could be worse than
losing you."

—Austin Lounge Lizards

CHAPTER NINE

ONE WEEK later, at four forty-five in the morning, I was loitering in the parking lot of a convenience store on the outskirts of Tedious, Texas, watching a large Hispanic male projectile-vomiting on the only pay phone in the place. At 5 A.M., according to the plan Lana Nelson and I had hammered out, I was to call my friend and contact man, Doug Holloway, who was then to pick me up and take me to meet the bus. As I gazed at the pay phone glistening in the chill moonlight, I began to wonder at the wisdom of the plan. But, like the Charge of the Light Brigade or the Mondale-Ferraro campaign, there was to be no turning back.

Winnie Katz, with unexpected graciousness, had taken responsibility for looking after the cat, even agreeing to let her reside for an indeterminate amount of time in her studio. "The cat belongs here," I remembered her saying, "with all the other girls." Then the two of them had watched with pity in their eyes as I walked out into the cold world and left them behind in that secret sanctum of Sapphos. I thought of all the reasons to be in New York and all the reasons not to be in New York and the only images that remained indelibly were the eyes of the cat burning brightly in my soul like the stars in the Texas sky.

Soon my queasiness gave way to mere uneasiness, and by dawn's surly light I made the call. Doug Holloway said he'd be right over and about half a century later, with his ponytail riding the night wind, he pulled into the parking lot driving a wayward golf cart.

"My BMW's in the shop," Doug said.

"Nothing serious, I hope."

"Nothing's been serious for a long time now," said Doug, as I hopped aboard and we shot silently through the night toward Willie's place, the golf cart hugging every curve in the country road.

"Jesus Christ," I said, "what do you have in this thing?"

"It's powered by the love of God and country and the best marijuana money can buy," he said as he took out a joint the size of a small Japanese torpedo. He fired it up with a lighter that had a flame not dissimilar in shape and coloration to that of a welder's torch. He took a huge hit and passed it over to me.

"No, thanks," I said. "I had an apple on the train."

I'd had a number of bad experiences with drugs, one of them lasting for several decades. I'd never been real partial to pot in the first place; it either nodded me out or led to rather unpleasant repercussions and sometimes it had both effects simultaneously. If I was going to get in trouble with a drug, at least I wanted to know about it while it was going on. In fact, my worst experience with pot was once back when Christ was a cowboy when I'd smoked some very high-powered boogitty weed with Willie on the bus just before I went onstage in front of fifty thousand people at a giant Farm Aid Concert in which the entire audience looked like giant ants, many of whom were wearing giant cowboy hats.

We scooted along in the darkness for another mile or two and then hooked a sharp right in between two Stonehenge-like boulders that stood at the gates of Briarcliff, Willie's sprawling former country-club outlaw getaway. Doug was halfway through the maze of little streets and halfway up a hill when the golf cart's little heart gave out.

"Motherfucker!" he shouted. "That's American engineering for you."

"Nothing serious, I hope," I said, as Doug leaped sideways out of the vehicle and began circling it like a highly Africanized bee.

Holloway did not reply to me, though he did have a few more words for the golf cart. I watched stoically for a few moments, then began unloading my Borracho de Vagina luggage. Soon the two of us, like brigands in the night, were marching up the long hill that ran along Willie's private golf course.

"It's par for the course," said Doug Holloway grimly. "And I mean that literally."

"It's not an auspicious start," I agreed.

"Some journeys that begin with rather humble origins," said Doug, "can often proceed to fuck up your life really bad."

"Life being what it is," I said, "how would anybody know?"

To paraphrase Bob Dylan, we walked ten thousand miles in the mouth of a golf course. At last, as we cleared a small bluff and the Beverly Hills designer colors of the dawn came creeping into my left iris, we could see Willie's tour bus standing alone in a little clearing. An Alamo on wheels. Even cynical eyes like my own, weary from the road, jaded from the city, clouded by the love I've left behind, had to admit that this particular bus in this particular dawn made a pure and powerful and singularly poignant picture.

My own country music career had never quite reached the tour-bus level. The closest I came was a blue Beauville van out of which the Texas Jewboys poured like *A Thousand Clowns* at every honky-tonk, minstrel show,

whorehouse, bar, and bar mitzvah throughout the South,
to paraphrase Jerry Jeff Walker. The Beauville, like my
career, was not a vehicle destined for vastly commercial
country music stardom. In size and stature it was somewhere between Willie's bus and the dysfunctional golf cart.
But it had, I reflected, at least one good quality. It broke
down at all the right places.

The Baby Jesus, I figured, had never wanted me to
have my own tour bus. No doubt He had other plans for
me. Maybe someday He'd like to share them. Of course,
Willie Nelson looked a lot like Jesus on a bad-hair day.
Maybe I'd just ask him.

I thanked Doug Holloway and headed down the hill
in the direction of the bus. In the onrushing colors of
dawn a strange mix of feelings were mingling in my mind.
Part of me was very excited by the prospect of travelling
across America with Willie. But part of me was remembering ruefully the decades of my life in which I'd toiled
futilely after success like some men toil after virtue. To
paraphrase Charles Lamb. I'd also experienced my share
of one-night stands, sawdust on the floor, club owners,
crowds staying away in droves, miles of meaningless highway with Negroes and Heebie-Jeebies and Rednecks and
cranked-up feminists angrily pursuing the Texas Jewboys
because we'd held up a little mirror reflecting some of
America's blind spots. To put it on a bumper sticker, I'd
been on the road so long that I'd come to hate the sound
of the human voice singing.

As I now approached the bus I had in mind something the great jazz drummer Buddy Rich had said just
before he'd died in a hospital bed some years ago.

"Is there anything making you uncomfortable, Mr.
Rich?" the nurse had reportedly asked.

"Yes," Rich had said. "Country music."

CHAPTER TEN

WHEN WILLIE NELSON is on the road again, which is almost all the time, his tour bus, the Honeysuckle Rose, becomes almost like a floating city unto itself. Floating, of course, is the operative word here. Even the secondhand smoke has been known to make casual visitors mildly amphibious. Though Willie does have three tour buses, there is no truth to the widely held belief that he needs the other two buses to carry all the weed he smokes on the first bus.

Actually, one bus is for the band, one is for the stage crew and equipment, and one is probably just about as close as Willie Nelson ever gets to being home. In Austin, they say that when you die you go to Willie Nelson's house. As I boarded the Honeysuckle Rose for points unknown, I had to admit I was damned lucky to have gotten there without having to step on a rainbow. I was also fairly fortunate, I reflected, to have gotten out of New York without falling through the trapdoor and waking up next to Oscar Wilde.

It had been almost five years since I'd spent any length of time travelling on the bus with the Red Headed Stranger and his musical and spiritual family of veteran gypsy souls. At that time I'd been researching a tabloid piece for *Rolling Stone* magazine about a woman who claimed that Willie had hosed her for nine consecutive hours on January 4, 1985 at the Biloxi, Mississippi, Hilton.

She also claimed that Nelson had performed something of a backward somersault at the end of the marathon act with her body still attached. Far from being grateful or at least appreciative of the experience, she was suing Nelson for fifty million dollars for breach of promise in refusing to marry her.

"I'm not saying it didn't happen," Willie had told me at the time. "It might've happened. But you would've thought I'd remember at least the first four or five hours."

"What will you do," I'd asked him, "if the case actually comes to court?"

Willie had thought for a moment and then he'd smiled. "My ex-wife Shirley said she'd be glad to testify on my behalf," he'd told me.

But that was all yesterday's wine. Recent years had also brought more serious troubles to Willie. The tragic suicide of his son in Nashville. The IRS lawsuit against him for over sixteen million dollars. The changing landscape of country music that now made major record-label support and generous radio air play almost a thing of the past. For many major legends of country music this trendy tidal wave toward modern youthful "hat acts" plus the inevitable pull of the old rocking chair had meant the end of careers it was once believed would last forever. And in the midst of all this, like a diamond amongst the rhinestones, Willie Nelson stays on the road.

The Honeysuckle Rose was a ghost town that morning. For some reason it felt like I was walking up the aisle of an empty church forever searching, in the words of Billy Joe Shaver, for "the Jesus of my choosin'." The only erect figures I could see were the chessmen standing mutely on Willie's little table, waiting to be touched by the hand of man or fate. I moved a pawn to king four and moved my own body, no doubt a pawn in someone else's game, back toward the sleeping compartment of the bus. All the bunks were empty. I threw my stuff on one of the bunks and walked stealthily back toward the closed door to Willie's private bedroom and inner sanctum. I didn't want to knock at that hour of the morning. He could be sleeping, writing, meditating, or, very possibly, hosing some woman from the Biloxi, Mississippi, Hilton.

I put my head close to the door and listened. Someone seemed to be moving around back there. As an amateur private detective, I'd spent a lot of time listening at a lot of closed doors. If you listen at a closed door long enough it'll usually tell you something you don't really want to know. It can also turn you into something you don't really want to be. Of course, sooner or later, whether we listen at closed doors or not, most of us turn into something we don't want to be anyway. There can only be so many artists in this world at any one time. As Rambam had once told me: "Every drunk is not a poet, Kinky." Now that I thought about it, that was probably the main reason I'd left New York and found myself down here listening at a closed door in the first place.

I turned to go back to the front of the bus and precisely at that moment the door swung open. Into the narrow darkened hallway of the bus stepped a vaguely sinister figure wraithed in long grayish hair and beard. It looked like Willie Nelson might look after spending a fortnight in an opium den with Sherlock Holmes.

It was Ben Dorsey, Willie's valet and personal caretaker, sometimes known as the World's Oldest Band Boy. Before working for Willie, Ben had been John Wayne's valet, a fact that did not take long to emerge in casual conversation with Dorsey. He looked enough like Willie to the untrained eye that Ben had done stand-in work for him in several movies.

"Ben," I said in some surprise. "What are you doing back there?" As far as I knew, almost no one was allowed into Willie's private sanctum.

"I have this thing, Kinky," said Ben. "It's called a job. What're you doin' back here?"

"Willie invited me down for a little R & R. Just to get out of New York a bit and travel with you guys."

"Well, it ain't a good time to be travelin' with us," said Ben. "There's been some mysterious things happenin'.

"Such as?"

"Willie invited you along," said Ben. "Why don't you ask him yourself?"

That, however, appeared to be a little difficult at the moment. Gator, the driver, had just gotten on the bus and, with a cheery "All aboard!", had started things off with a lurch.

Willie was nowhere to be seen.

CHAPTER ELEVEN

DON'T LISTEN to Ben," said Gator, as I sat up front and watched the highway roll. Ben was back somewhere in the kitchen puttering around like a mad scientist, muttering constantly about fried-egg sandwiches, upon which Nelson, apparently, largely subsisted. Ben had already removed my luggage to another bunk, contending that was where L.G. slept. L.G. was Willie's one-man security team. I wasn't going to argue with him.

"Ben just sees things that aren't there sometimes," Gator continued.

"Like Willie Nelson, for instance," I said. "Where the hell is he?"

"Oh, we'll pick Willie and Bobbie and L.G. up in Abbott. It's right on the way to Fort Worth. We're playin' Billy Bob's tonight. Unless, of course, Willie has other ideas."

"Does he often have other ideas?"

Gator laughed. "If Willie decides to turn this bus around and head for Peru, that's where we'll go."

"Have you driven him there before?"

"Several times," said Gator with a smile. "But that was long ago. Willie decides where he wants to go. My job is to see that he gets there. Ben's job is to see that he has plenty of fried-egg sandwiches."

"There's certainly a clearly defined delegation of authority."

"And if there's one thing we won't stand for around here it's authority," said Gator.

Gator, whose real name was Gates Moore, was a friendly, good-looking, easygoing guy who drove a route sometimes that many a blue-ball trucker couldn't handle. From past road trips I liked Gator. I also liked L.G. I even got along with Ben Dorsey sometimes.

"You know Willie," said Gator, as the Hill Country scenery flashed by like a kaleidoscope. "He's a gypsy."

There was that word again. I gazed ahead in silence through the big windshield as the Honeysuckle Rose snorted up the endless lines of the highway. Aside from the little town of Abbott and the big honky-tonk known as Billy Bob's, I wondered, not for the first time, exactly where the hell I was going.

Abbott, Texas, was such a small place it looked like a good storm could wash it away, which was not a fortuitous thing, because by the time we got there it was raining like hell. One dark night at the end of April 1933, Willie Nelson had been born here. In May of that year, Jimmie Rodgers, the legendary Singin' Brakeman, had died of TB in New York City, thus establishing a certain cosmic linkage between the two country music greats, but at the same time making it rather difficult for Rodgers ever to perform on a duet album with Nelson.

I was looking at a boarded-up country store in the rain and thinking about New York when Gator gave the bus a savage swing to the right and I almost swallowed my cigar. We were now barreling down a small country road that seemed more like a green-gray tunnel under the canopy of the trees and the rain.

"This little street," said Gator, as he slowed the bus slightly, "is where Willie was born."

"Very nice," I said. It was impossible to see anything but rain.

As I tried to visually penetrate the slanting veil of gray, I heard a strange voice singing very softly close to my left ear.

"*'I have often walked down this street before.*
But the pavement always stayed beneath my
feet before. . . .'"

I turned and looked up to see the face of Ben Dorsey. There was a smile on the face but the eyes were, for that instant, very definitely the eyes of a madman.

"Another side of Ben Dorsey," said Gator, as he stopped the bus and opened the door to a cold torrent of rain.

In a matter of moments Willie and his sister Bobbie were aboard the bus, followed quickly by the large tattooed form of L.G. With L.G. standing behind them, Willie and Bobbie looked like little gingerbread people, inherently good, almost magical, and somehow, it seemed, fragile beyond words and music. Then the door closed. Then the bus began to roll. Then we were on the road again.

"Here's something you might like to hear," said Willie, as he motioned me over to the little table and slotted a cassette into the bus's stereo system. "You and I might do a good job on this one together."

I knew what the song was even before it began playing. It was written by Ned Sublett and was something that had come into Willie's hands years ago. Ever since, he and I had sent versions back and forth and entertained the notion of recording the rather sick song. The title of the piece was "Cowboys Are Frequently Secretly Fond of Each Other."

Now, as it played over the speakers, Willie tilted his head to one side as if listening in a rapture.

"You know," he said, "you and I really oughtta record this son of a bitch."

"I live in hope," I said, winking at Bobbie.

"You know, the old house we were born in isn't there anymore," said Willie, jumping to a new subject with all the adroitness of a man in a mental hospital.

"Willie built a new one," said Bobbie, "but they tore the original one down before we even knew about it. We were on the road somewhere when they did it."

"Now, about that song . . ." I interjected.

"They did manage to save the bedroom I was born in," said Willie, taking out a joint roughly the size and shape of an old-fashioned rural butane tank. He lit it up and inhaled deeply.

"What did they do with it?" I asked, giving up the ghost.

"What did they do with what?" Willie said. He held the joint out to me, his eyes sparkling like stars.

"What did they do with the bedroom you were born in?" I said. I took the joint and took a hit. Hell, I thought, I was off duty. I couldn't remember if I'd ever actually been on duty.

"They moved it across town," said Willie. "I think a black family's livin' in it."

I looked briefly out the window at the rain. It was falling softer now on the shoulder of the highway.

"There goes the neighborhood," I said.

CHAPTER TWELVE

WANDERING AROUND backstage at a Willie Nelson concert is a bit like being the parrot on the shoulder of the guy who's running the ferris wheel. It's not the best seat in the house, but you see enough lights, action, people, and confusion to make you wonder if anybody knows what the hell's really going on. If you're sitting out front, of course, the show rolls along as smoothly as a German train schedule, but as Willie Nelson, like any great magician, would be the first to point out, the real show is never in the center ring.

Backstage at any show, whether it's Broadway, or the circus, or the meanest little honky-tonk in Nacogdoches, Texas, has its similarities. The palpable sense of people out there somewhere in the darkness waiting for your performance. Or, if you really have pawnshop balls, pulling a curtain back slightly and experiencing the actual sight of the audience sitting there waiting to be entertained by someone who, in this case, happens to be you. The little things you think about or don't think about in order to get ready when the man says "Five minutes, Mr. Jolson."

It's the reason Richard Burton vomited before almost every live performance of his life. It's part of the reason George Jones took Early Times, Judy Garland took bluebirds, and many a brightly shining star burned out too soon. Standing alone in the spotlight, up on the high wire without a net, is something Willie Nelson has had to deal with for most of his adult life. Does he have any special tricks he uses? Does he ever get nervous? I was curious, but I didn't want to ask him any hard questions just before the show. So I continued wandering around backstage. After all, I was America's guest.

Willie's crew looked like a band of gypsies who'd just broken into a Rolex distributorship. Most of them were familiar to me and many of them were friendly, but all of them looked busy. It was nearing showtime and as Ben Dorsey had said, they had this thing that was called a job. I was able to say hello to Poodie Locke, who was Willie's stage manager and to prove it had the longest pigtail in the crowd. Willie had met Poodie on the gangplank of Noah's Ark, standing just behind Paul English, Willie's drummer. Poodie was balancing on top of a small mountain of speaker equipment, shouting instructions into a walkie-talkie.

"How's it look tonight, Poodie?" I asked, when he saw me and waved me over.

"The same way it's looked every fucking night for the past twenty-five years," he said. "Fortunately we're not in control."

The atmosphere seemed to be getting a bit more frenzied in the wings, so I drifted over to the dressing room and noticed it was filling up with local celebrities and slightly over-the-hill groupies, better known in Nashville as snuff queens. The ebb and flow of riffraff gave the place an aura not dissimilar to that of a Christian Science reading room during happy hour.

In one corner I noticed Larry Trader, an old friend of Willie's and a promoter who'd once helped my band, the Texas Jewboys, escape a redneck lynch mob in East Texas. Larry, of course, had been the one who'd booked the gig there in the first place, but I'd been the one who'd had the misjudgment to try to perform it.

"Jesus Christ," I said, "does he always draw this many blind people and folks in wheelchairs? It looks like an old-time revival show."

"Will's not a doctor," said Trader with a laugh. "But he is a healer through music. It does have a bit of that old-time revival feel to it, doesn't it?"

"Yeah," I said, swigging a Lone Star and gazing languorously out a side door at the crowd of expectant believers.

"Now if he could just revive you and me," said Trader, "everything'd be fine."

The band was doing some final tuning up and so I tuned out and phased over to a backstage area that appeared to have a nice spread laid out along with liquor drinks for the heat. I traded the Lone Star longneck in for a long shot of Jack Daniel's and a Dr. Pecker on the side. With a glass in each hand I wandered over to the stage area but still out of view of the crowd. I was standing there in near darkness smoking a cigar and alternating slugs from each glass, which is no little feat, as it were, when a voice right behind me almost caused me to drop my cigar into my Dr. Pecker.

"Let me show you something," it said.

It was Willie Nelson with his guitar around his neck and wearing his high-rodeo drag performance outfit, which, in his case, was jeans, a T-shirt, tennis shoes, and a bandanna. Ben Dorsey probably didn't have to bust his buttocks working as Willie's valet.

Willie pulled a stage curtain back slightly, keeping us in semidarkness yet revealing a cranked-up crowd beginning to get drunk, beginning to grow restless, and packed into Billy Bob's tighter than smoked oysters in Hong Kong. Viewed from our hidden angle they were a strangely intimidating sight, yet Willie took them in almost like a walk in the trailer park.

"That's where the real show is," he said.

"If that's where the real show is," I said, "I want my money back."

"Do you realize," Willie continued in a soft, soothing, serious voice, "that ninety-nine percent of those people are not with their true first choice?"

"Do you realize," I said, "that you and I aren't with our true first choice either? I mean a latent homosexual relationship is a nice thing to have going for us, but sooner or later—"

But Willie wasn't listening to my tissue of horseshit cocktail chatter. If anything, he was busy taking Joan of Arc lessons himself. He looked out at the crowd for a moment or two longer then he let the curtain drop from his hand, sending us back into twilight.

"That's why they play the jukebox," he said.

CHAPTER THIRTEEN

GOVERNMENTS, entire civilizations, even fast-food franchises can rise and fall in the time Willie Nelson routinely devotes to signing autographs after a show. In fairness to Willie, he always seems to bring the even-mindedness of the old Mahatma to the operation along with a genuine interest in each and every fan. This is not true of all celebrities and entertainers. When the mother of one of the Knicks basketball players approached Bill Cosby for an autograph after a game, he told her: "We'll get back to you." Even worse, according to the *National Enquirer,* which is as accurate a beacon of truth as any in this hall of mirrors we call the modern world, is the recent behavior of Barry Antelope. Antelope had just finished a concert in Florida and, unlike Willie, had refused all requests to sign autographs. When an overly zealous female fan caught up with his limo and presented him with her little autograph book, he wrote in it the following sensitive message: "Stay the fuck away from me. Barry Antelope." God only knows what John Denver and Alan Alda are really like.

The show itself had been killer bee, verging at moments upon the hypnotic. Now, the extended love-in with the fans provided me with the opportunity to renew old acquaintances with the band and crew who would be my road companions in the days ahead. To my mild surprise, I found myself missing McGovern and Rambam and

Chinga and even Ratso. In fact, I found myself missing
both Ratsos, New York and Washington. Washington
Ratso, I'd recently learned, was a charter member of a
small rather arcane organization called the Men's Titanic
Society. They celebrated the chivalry of the men who went
down on the *Titanic* and hoped to imbue today's society
with that kind of courage and sense of honor. They had
their work cut out for them, I figured.

All this not withstanding, in the manner of a homesick
young camper back at Echo Hill, I fought down my emo-
tions, and ventured forth into a brave new world popu-
lated by equally colorful characters, often with equally
absurd animal names. Not only did Gator and Poodie work
for Willie, but over the years such creatures as Snake,
Beast, Bee, and Pooh-Bah had wandered in and out of the
gypsy caravan. I'd gravitated to people with strange animal
names even before I was Kinky. Just because I'd been
miserable for forty-nine years was no reason to change
horses in the middle of the stream.

I walked back to the dressing rooms and found
Willie's harp player, Mickey Raphael, wrapping up the
exchange of phone numbers and hobbies with three attractive young bubbettes at the same time as he was wrapping up about eighty-seven harmonicas of various and
somewhat Freudian shapes and sizes.

"Don't forget, Mickey," giggled one of the girls as
they left the dressing room, "call me when y'all come to
Lubbock."

"Are you going to call her?" I said, after the trio had
exited.

"Might as well," he said. "There's nothing else to do
in Lubbock."

"You could visit Buddy Holly's grave," I suggested, as
I grabbed a Pearl beer out of a nearby cooler.

"I already do that, Kinkster," said Mickey. "Every night I'm on the road."

It was true, I reflected, that the road had a way of killing you so slowly and subtly that after a while you didn't even know you were dead. You didn't even want to know. The highway would put you to bed at night. The hotel would wake you up in the morning. Someone would see that your guitar or your luggage got where it was going and most of the time you got there, too. Maybe some day you'd find yourself in Lubbock and maybe you'd call if you still had the number and you still could remember who'd given it to you.

"Maybe you need a break," I said. "Get off the road. Join the Shalom Retirement Village People for a while."

Mickey Raphael looked around the dressing room with a bit more furtiveness than seemed entirely necessary. Then he moved very close to me.

"You know," I said, "you're not an unattractive young man."

"I'll call you when I'm in New York," he said. "But it's not me that needs a break. The one I'm worried about is Willie."

"What are you talking about? Willie seems just like Willie. That was one of the best shows I've ever seen tonight."

"Oh, I know. He's the great stone face. It's nothing anyone could see unless they've worked with him every night. I tell you, he's deeply troubled about something and it's just not like him to be that way."

"Maybe it's trouble with Annie."

Annie was Willie's ninety-seventh wife, and even if she'd been June Cleaver she'd be having some kind of trouble being married to Willie Nelson. On the other hand, as Hank Williams used to say, they had a license to fight.

"You forget," said Mickey, "that I've been through more than a few wives with Willie, not to mention the IRS taking my fucking harmonicas, and a lot worse shit than that, but I've never seen him this way before. And I'm not the only one who's noticed this in him. Everybody's noticed it. If I didn't know better I'd say he seems haunted by something."

"Look, Mick. Willie invited me on this tour because I thought *I* was snappin' my wig and now you're telling me you think *he's* snappin' his wig."

"And as long as you're here, you might as well do some amateur sleuthing and try to find out what's troubling him so badly. You know he'll never tell anybody."

"Hold the weddin'. That's a whole other help line. I'm not a fucking shrink. I'm not even a licensed PI. I'm just here as a friend."

"That's why you're the one that has to do it. You're not his lawyer or his accountant. You're not on the payroll working for him. You're his friend. So be a friend."

"I wouldn't know where to start."

"You can start by talking to Just Bill. Willie's been spending a lot of time with him lately. You can tell him Groucho sent you."

"Just Bill? What's his full name?"

"Just Bill," said Mickey.

CHAPTER FOURTEEN

IN ORDER to get a second opinion, or possibly a third if you wanted to count Ben Dorsey's, I grabbed another Pearl and drifted around the backstage area. Willie, I noticed, was still out front smiling, signing autographs, and posing for pictures, a sizable crowd still milling around him like a friendly lynch mob. Everyone else in North America seemed to be backstage, which made it difficult for me to unobtrusively walk up to people and ask them if they thought Willie Nelson could conceivably be cookin' on another planet.

I caught sight of Paul English, who'd known Willie about as long as anybody except for sister Bobbie, but he seemed in somewhat of a hurry. Paul appeared to be locked in a heated discussion with Bee Spears, the bass player, as both of them beat a path toward the area behind Billy Bob's where the buses were parked. It's been my experience that drummers, usually the craziest people in bands, and bass players, usually the most tedious people, seem to spend a lot of time together offstage and seem to agree upon almost nothing. On this occasion all I got from the two of them was a casual little papal wave from Bee and a mildly satanic smile from Paul. But it would keep, I figured. The nice thing about being on the road again was that sooner or later you always caught up with everybody.

One of the ones I caught up with sooner was Jody

Payne, Willie's guitar player, who was putting his ax into its case as if he were laying a child in a casket.

"Where'd you first meet Willie?" I said, as Jody was snapping shut his guitar case.

"It was nineteen sixty-two in Detroit," said Jody, who would've made a good government witness because he could miraculously remember everything. "It was at the West Fort Tavern. Willie sat in for a few songs and sang 'Half a Man,' which practically blew me away. Then the owner of the bar came over to me and said: 'Don't let him sing no more. He's the worst singer I've ever heard in my life.'"

"That's the same thing the voice coach once told Enrico Caruso."

"Who'd he play with?" said Jody.

"Clayton Delaney," I said, as Jody picked up his guitar case and I picked up a bottle of Shiner's dark beer. "Look, Jody," I said, "just between you and me and Lefty Frizzell, have you noticed any changes in Willie lately?"

Jody put his guitar case on the floor. A mildly troubled expression crossed his cheerful face.

"I know you're a friend of his, so I'll tell you this. Hell yes, he's been different of late. I mean I know all his tricks. When I first met him he was playing bass for Ray Price and Willie was so clever that it took Ray almost six months to realize that Willie couldn't play bass. It took me about five minutes. But this time I'm completely thrown. Something's eatin' him real bad and he won't even admit it."

Something was eatin' all of us pretty bad, I thought, and we didn't want to admit it either. It was a little thing called life and it probably wasn't going to stop eating us until there was nothing left but a cat pissing on the postcard you left in the secret pocket of your childhood. Yes, ma'am, life was going to eat us all alive, all right. Then it was going to order a crème brûlée and maybe an afterdinner drink. Then it was going to walk the check.

"Hey," Jody Payne was saying, "you been doing some pretty fair crime solving up there in New York. Why don't you try your hand at solving this one here on the road?"

"I don't have a client," I said.

For the next half an hour I worked the house a bit backstage but failed to shed any light on Willie's current state of mental hygiene. So what if certain members of Willie's family found him to be a bit nervous, short-tempered, and unfocused of late? Maybe that's what happens to you after a lifetime on the road working 365 shows a year smoking seven rain forests full of hemp and running into some drunken, long-forgotten, hostile high school bullet-head at every gig who refuses to let go of your hand and keeps saying to you: "What's my name? You don't even remember my name, do you? Sumbitch don't even know my name. What's my name? Tell me my name!"

I'll tell you your name, I thought. Your name is Unpleasant. Your name is Tedious. Bubba Tedious Unpleasant Fuckhead. Am I right? But Willie would never have told him that. Not the Willie I knew.

On the way down the hallway leading out to the buses I passed a small room where some local radio guy was taping an interview with Bobbie Nelson. Bobbie and I were kindred souls and she waved to me like a little girl from a long-ago classroom in grade school. Maybe I'd talk to her later about this business and maybe I wouldn't. Maybe I'd just let the whole matter remain in Willie's head along with a lot of other matters that weren't any of my business. On the other hand, inquiring minds wanted to know and, once they found out, very possibly, crucify you with knitting needles.

In the parking lot of Billy Bob's I ran into Lana Nel-

son along with Doug Holloway and Sammy Allred of Gee-
zinslaw Brothers fame. Sammy and Doug had driven up
from Austin for the show, and Lana, of course, had been
on the road with Daddy ever since she'd finished jumping
rope in the schoolyard, which was a measure of maturity
that Sammy, Doug, and I had so far failed to attain. Lana
had a fashionably dressed, very good-looking young man
with her who seemed to manifest a rather well-defined
aura of spiritual slumming, which was not all that hard to
do in Billy Bob's parking lot.

"Howdy," he said, with a fish handshake all around.
"Just visiting Texas and I thought I'd catch a Willie show.
He's the greatest, isn't he? He never quits."

"Trevor's an actor in Hollywood," said Lana.

"Really?" said Sammy. "What restaurant?"

CHAPTER FIFTEEN

IF YOU PLAY enough one-night stands, sooner or later you'll find that everywhere you go and everyone you know has become just another station on the way. On the way to where is, by this time, something you know even less about than you did when your journey started. But you feel like you have to keep going even if it kills you and, of course, in one way or another, it always does.

By 1976, after four rugged years on the road with the Texas Jewboys and many months performing as part of Bob Dylan's Rolling Thunder Revue, I'd pretty much become a perpetual case of wake me when we get there if we're goin'. Exhaustion, ennui, and a passenger train full of Peruvian marching powder had pressed a triple crown of thorns deep into my gray-matter department, and I was still waiting for my soul to come back from the dry cleaner in the town we'd left behind.

I had become an applause junkie. A performing seal, flying on eleven different kinds of herbs and spices, so high I needed a stepladder to scratch my ass, so high I was starting to feel lonely. I was a spinning ghost. A rambling hunchback, travelling from town to town waiting for my next hit. But it takes millions of years, I figured, to become the kind of star a lonely cricket can make a wish on.

Then one fine day on a deserted beach somewhere on Jalapa just off the coast of Mazatlán, I found myself walking and talking with another Jewboy. A Minnesota

Jewboy. It was a warm, tropical day but he kept his black leather jacket on the whole time. Maybe he felt a cold chill coming from somewhere too far away for anyone else to feel. Maybe it was the way of his people. If he'd ever had a reason for doing anything it was one he'd never reveal. Like Sherlock Holmes's reticence in explaining a case in progress, Bob Dylan was righteously cautious about unlocking the spiritual machinery that was his life. It was enough that he'd written: "She never stumbles / She's got no place to fall."

By the time we got to that distant beach I'd been travelling with Bob for about eleven months and it felt like a year. Rolling Thunder had covered more territory than Willy Loman or the seminal expeditions of the sixteenth-century Italian explorer Clitorius Ferrero. Bob Dylan had probably played for more people than the Pope. Of course, every now and then one Pope croaks and another Pope steps up to the communion wafer plate and white and black smoke rises from the Vatican and, depending upon which it is, they either kneel and pray or dance around and sing "The Wicked Witch Is Dead."

But there's only one Bob Dylan, and if he ever stumbled he was going to take a lot of people and a big slice of musical history with him, not to mention a phalanx of promoters, an army of accountants, a legion of lawyers, and a constellation of critics from *The New York Times,* not to mention my friend Tommy Masters, who drives the bus.

"I once knew a gypsy king," Bob was saying. "Travelled around with him in Spain."

"Never been to Spain," I said.

"He had ten wives and over a hundred children—"

"At five bucks a pop, that's almost enough for a second show."

"And there was a young boy who was kind of mystical,

sort of an idiot-savant. He could catch a fly with his bare hands. He'd move his hand very slowly and he'd always catch the fly."

"A fly like in baseball or a fly like the one Emily Dickinson heard when she died?"

Dylan ignored this question. Of course, Dylan, as a general rule, ignored all questions.

"Anyway, I came back on the road for a while and then, some years later, went back to Spain and visited the king again. This time he was all alone."

"He'd gone acoustic?"

"The wives had drifted away as he'd become older and weaker and so had the children. He had only one wagon left of the many he'd once owned. I rode with him in that wagon. It was a lonely ride."

"What finally happened to the gypsy king?"

Bob did not answer right away. Like the sad-eyed lady of the lowlands, he seemed to be watching gypsy wagons rolling along on the breakers far out at sea.

"When you die," he said at last, "they let you off the hook."

Bob Dylan and Willie Nelson had been like spiritual bookends for the musical and possibly mystical, if dusty, shelves of my life. They both know what it's like to be gypsy kings. They also know how deafening and spirit-grinding loneliness can be once you've been king of the gypsies. I look up to both of them for wisdom and advice even though they're both shorter than anyone except Paul Simon.

But I wouldn't for any reason try to get inside either of their heads. Once I'd gotten there, a small hand might try to catch me, moving very slowly, like the windmill wheels of a gypsy wagon.

CHAPTER SIXTEEN

BY THE TIME I got a chance to talk to Just Bill it was two days later and he was spit-polishing the headlights of the Honeysuckle Rose on a cold night out back of the Oklahoma City Holiday Inn. The Holiday Inn was Willie Nelson's favorite hotel for two reasons. One was that you didn't have to enter through the lobby. The other reason was that at a Holiday Inn there were supposed to be "no surprises." Most of the time, however, the hotels were only used by the band and the stage crew, with Willie only darkening the side or rear doors of the places on special occasions such as semiannual showers. In fact, if Willie Nelson had been Rosa Parks there probably never would have been a civil rights movement in America because he definitely would've insisted upon staying in the back of the bus.

"Do your friends call you 'Just,' " I said, as I puffed a cigar in the darkness, "or do they call you Bill?"

"Just Bill," said Just Bill.

I absorbed the information as if it were something I needed to think about for a while. For his part, Just Bill never even looked up. Since the bus was parked in the northern hemisphere, he continued polishing the headlights in a practiced, meticulous, clockwise motion. While Just Bill did not appear to be the overly forthcoming type, one of the advantages of being Willie's invited guest on a road tour was that everyone tried to be at least next door to civil to you whether they liked you or not. Just Bill was no doubt doing his best to be an accommodating host. I was doing my best not to be a repellent guest. It was also true that Willie had so many friends from so many different casinos of experience that no one could say for sure who really knew the man longer or better. This created a certain jockeying among some for what they felt might be the inside track. Those who knew Willie well realized that trying to figure out what was going on in the man's head would always be a loser's game.

"Look," I said, "it's probably none of my damn business and if you don't want to talk about it it's fine with me. But Ben's been hinting to me for several days that something strange is going on and Mickey Raphael says Willie's off his feed for some reason and I wondered if you cared to shed some light on it."

"Never heard of a cop named Kinky."

"I'm not a cop. I'm a private investigator." Even that was pushing it, I thought, but it sounded better than nosy bastard from New York.

Just Bill stood up and looked me over as if he were giving me serious consideration for the job of assistant headlight washer. He didn't seem to be too knocked out with what he saw.

"I'm also Willie's friend," I said.

"Well," said Just Bill, "Ben's right. So's Mickey. I just don't know what there is you and I can do about it."

"Well, you can start by telling me when you first noticed whatever it is you noticed."

"Oh, that part's easy. But I don't want anything I tell you gettin' back to Willie."

"That part's easy, too. It'll be our little secret." I smiled in the darkness thinking of my friend Ted Mann's line: "The only secrets the Kinkster's ever kept are the

ones he's forgotten." I couldn't remember whether or not
it was true.

"It all started about two months ago," said Just Bill,
"when Gator runned over the Indian."

"That'll do it every time," I said. "Care to amplify?"

"Well, it wasn't Gator's fault, you see. He was haulin'
ass through the Arizona desert late one night on the way
to the next gig and this drunk old Indian just steps out on
the highway right in front of the bus."

"I understand. The bus didn't have a drunken-Indian
guard."

"There was nothin' he could've done. But it was bad,
you see. Hit Willie almost as hard as it hit the Indian. He's
part Indian too, you know."

I nodded. Sooner or later, I thought, we're all going
to be Indians. Just give it a little time. I listened as Just
Bill continued his story in somewhat graphic detail.

"I never seen so much blood, guts, and feathers in
my life. It was just like Big Bird flew into the windshield.
Hell of a mess."

"Must've made your job a bit harder."

"Damn straight. Took me about a week to wash the
bus and I was still findin' little bacon-sized strips in the
grillwork. It wasn't pretty, I can tell you that. Sheriff's
deputies were swarming all over the place. But L.G. and
the sheriff huddled together and signed a bunch of papers
and talked it all over for a few hours. Gator was pretty
shook up, of course, but not as shook up as Willie. Willie's
face looked white as a sheet. And that's pretty unusual
for a guy who's part Indian. Did I tell you Willie's part
Indian?"

"I believe you mentioned that in passing."

"Well, he is, and I think he thinks this accident could
bring about some kind of bad luck or bad karma or some
weird plague right out of the Bible, you see."

"The biblical plague's already happened. It was called the IRS."

"Yeah, but the accident itself wasn't the end of it. Turns out this guy we hit was some kind of medicine man of the tribe."

"Jesus Christ."

"That's what Willie said. Only he mentioned his middle name, too."

"H.?" I said.

"No," said Just Bill. "Fuckin'."

I thanked Just Bill and started to wander off. If a spiritual guy like Willie was nervous in the service, this sounded like a pretty damn good reason. I didn't get more than a few steps before Just Bill grabbed my arm.

"But that ain't the worst of it," he said. "There's more."

"I was afraid the other moccasin was going to drop."

"It sure as hell did. About two weeks after the accident we were playing a state fair somewhere in Florida, thousands of miles away, and a guy comes up to the bus after the show and he's got a little buckskin-wrapped package he wants to give to Willie. The guy's got coal black eyes and long pigtails just like Willie's, except they're black. He looks just like Kawliga come to life."

For those who are ignorant of Hank Williams's talents, "Kawliga" was one of the greatest, as well as one of the saddest, songs Hank ever wrote. Essentially, it deals with a wooden Indian who falls in love with an Indian maid "over in the antique store." One day a wealthy customer buys the Indian maid and takes her far away "but ol' Kawliga stayed." "Kawliga" is sad in the way that "Frosty the Snowman" is sad. But many people, especially some of those who work for record companies, don't see it that way. That's why my kid sister, Marcie, since she was a child, has kept an album cover from an old Hank Williams record on the wall of her room. The album is called "Kawliga and Other Humorous Songs." On the cover is one of the saddest pictures of Hank I've ever seen.

"So what was in the package the Indian gave to Willie?"

"Don't know," said Just Bill. "I saw him open it, look at it, and put it in his pocket."

"Did he say anything to you?"

"Yeah. He said that Indian we runned over was going to come back and find him. I asked Willie what he thought the dead Indian was going to do when he found him."

"What'd Willie say?"

"Willie said: 'Kill me, of course.'"

CHAPTER SEVENTEEN

WHILE I BELIEVED in old Indian legends and curses about as much as the next American who lived in a city with an Indian name, I recognized that it was not especially best foot forward to scoff at the notion. Several years ago while travelling in the Outback of Australia I found myself in a land that time had forgotten. I called the desk at my luxury hotel to inquire about which television channel carried CNN. The desk clerk said: "What, sir, is CNN?"

Later, before trekking across the Outback, I studied the list of things a white man would require to make the trip safely and then reviewed the items an Aboriginal would require to make the same trip. The white man needed the following things: sturdy hiking boots, large canteen with emergency supplies of water, first-aid kit, two-way radio, flashlight, tinned foods of every variety under the sun (that's why they needed to be tinned), broad-brimmed hat with hole punched in one side of the brim for two-way radio or walkie-talkie, gun and knife for protection in case you meet an idiot like yourself, maps of the area (though it hasn't really changed since Banjo Paterson wrote "Waltzing Matilda" in 1896), and emergency phone and fax numbers so that you can contact the nearest koala bear with a pager (though, of course, they're not really bears), and antisnake and antispider venom, though if you're bitten by the redback spider it's curtains on opening night. The female redback eats her mate, incidentally, during mating. The male redback, according to my friend Piers Akerman, has a corkscrew penis. This may account for the female redback's behavior. If you're bitten by the taipan snake, I'm afraid there won't be time to upgrade your software. The taipan denatures the blood, breaking it down totally and instantaneously. The taipan, they say in Australia, can kill a horse in half a second. That concludes the list of items the white man needs to survive in the Outback. The Aboriginal's list of necessities is much shorter, of course. In fact, it contains only one item: a stick.

During the time I travelled in the territory that surrounds Ayres Rock, or Uluru, as it's known to the Aboriginals, there was one ancient ritual that seemed to shed some light on what might now be happening to one of America's last living folk heroes, Willie Nelson. It explained how it might just be possible for the spirit of a dead Indian to return and destroy a living, breathing American who deeply venerated his Native American genesis. The Aboriginal rite I speak of is of a rather morbid nature. It is called "pointing the bone."

"Pointing the bone," a ritual that dates back thousands of years, is practiced very rarely, and then only by the maban-tjara or spiritual leader of an Aboriginal tribe. It is a mystical, infallible death warrant. If the leader points a certain sacred piece of broken bone at you, you will die. It's as simple as that. And death, invariably, will come within two or three days. Death comes from within and kills the victim in some arcane fashion the civilized world does not understand. The only prerequisite for the ritual to be effective is that the victim must truly believe that "pointing the bone" will kill him. And very few Aboriginals are doubting Thomases.

In our modern, more sophisticated society we do not

have a precise equivalent of "pointing the bone." Our culture, however, is not without its undeniable death warrants. When your doctor tells you that you have AIDS or inoperable cancer and you're going to die, you usually do. It may take you a little longer than the Aboriginal to reach what they call Dreamtime, but if you believe your doctor, you'll get there. Only occasionally does the patient override the doctor's grim incantations in our modern society. One example of this phenomenon was George Burns's almost religious insistence upon smoking cigars. On his one hundredth birthday, someone asked him what his doctor might say about his cigar smoking. "My doctor is dead," said Burns.

I wanted Willie Nelson to stay all night and stay a little longer. But Just Bill's strange tale was burning a gnarly little scenario in some unswept corner of my gray-matter department. Just Bill's version of events, of course, could all be a lot of horseshit and wild honey, but somehow I didn't think so. If Willie Nelson truly believed in something akin to "pointing the bone" and somebody was really aiming the thing at him, I was going to have a hell of a time trying to help him. It'd be like trying to save an angel flying too close to the ground.

CHAPTER EIGHTEEN

IT WAS two days later, around one o'clock in the morning, when I finally got a chance to talk alone with Willie over a fitful game of chess. The elapsed time since Just Bill had woven his morbid tale had given me an opportunity to think things through a bit in the pale, dying light of the twentieth century and now I felt somewhat reticent about asking Willie Nelson whether or not he believed he was the victim of an ancient Indian curse. Of course, when you're on a bus bound for Buffalo there are very few subjects, indeed, that you can't find the time or inclination to discuss.

"I'm far too self-absorbed," I said, "to notice behavioral change in others."

"Me, too," said Willie. "But you don't seem all that different."

In spite of my comment to Willie, I couldn't help but observe the difference in his chess game. He was usually a lightning-quick, instinctive player, but his game was now about as slow-moving as some people's dreams. His stage performances were still stellar, I reflected, but many great artists gave their greatest performances when they were literally dying inside. On the other hand, chess is a game of focus and concentration. As Edgar Allan Poe said, it is "complex without being profound." It is also a good index of a man's emotional state. A troubled mind will always declare itself in a game of chess. Of course, so will smoking a joint the size of a large kosher salami, though it'd never seemed to bother Willie in the past.

"I've been talking to some of the people close to you," I said, as delicately as I could put it. "They seem to feel that something's different about you recently but they don't know what it is."

"When they figure it out," said Willie, as he moved his knight, "I wish they'd let me know. Your move."

"My move," I said, "is to tell you I know about the accident."

"My move," said Willie, "is to tell you that there are no accidents." His eyes locking on to mine, seemed to be reflecting the very wisdom of the ages. In fact, the only eyes I'd seen that appeared to contain more wisdom belonged to my cat back in New York. There was no point in beating around the burning bush.

"The accident," I said, "where the Honeysuckle Rose T-boned the drunken Indian in Arizona."

"That was no accident," said Willie. "That was supposed to happen."

I got up from Willie's little table and paced back and forth a time or two in the aisle of the bus, smoking my cigar and thinking things over again. Dealing with a Zen Texan like Willie might be more difficult than I'd thought.

"Maybe it was supposed to *happen*," I said, "but it's not supposed to be this way. A few more little accidents like that could total anybody's karma—even yours. Especially if you let it destroy you."

"Nothing can destroy anything that doesn't want to be destroyed," said Willie, taking another long hit on the salami. "I don't believe in death. It's just part of life, part of country music. It's just like winning or losing a game of chess as you're moving through somebody else's time and space like the highwaymen on horseback painted on the back of this bus. How do you think *they* feel?"

"I'll ask them when we get to Buffalo."

I sat back down at the table and studied the chess-board. There were a number of ways to go, but none of them looked too promising. When all was said and done, life was very probably a stalemate, I reflected. Like win-ning or losing a game of chess as you're moving through somebody else's time and space.

"How'd you find out about it?" said Willie suddenly.

"You know us country singers-turned-amateur private investigators," I said. "We never reveal our sources. Now, maybe if you gave me two or three hundred."

"It doesn't really matter. It's just something I'd prefer not to see on *Hard Copy* if possible. Only five of us were on the bus at the time: L.G., Bobbie, me, Ben, and Gator, who had the misfortune of being behind the wheel. The other two buses were ahead of us and for a lot of reasons we decided to keep the incident strictly aboard the Hon-eysuckle Rose. I didn't even tell Paul or Poodie or anyone in the band or the rest of the family. It's my problem and there's no reason why everyone else should be bummed out just because I am."

Willie took another puff on the joint. I took a puff on the cigar. We stared at each other across a smoky chess-board that had suddenly become as meaningless as only life itself can sometimes seem.

"A few weeks went by," said Willie, "and I thought we had the whole nightmare pretty well behind us."

"Then the Indian showed up with the package wrapped in buckskin."

"You're a hell of a private dick, Big Dick."

"Mucous garcias," I said. "But it sounds like these may be some deep waters. Is there anything I can do?"

"Yeah," said Willie. "You can move your queen before I take it with my knight."

CHAPTER NINETEEN

As the frozen fingers of dawn filtered into the bus I was sitting up front on a cluttered couch trying to straighten out a wayward song lyric that was running relentlessly through my head. "It was a package show in Buffalo / It was us and Kitty Wells and Charley Pride. . . ." It was from an old Willie song, and one of my personal favorites, "Me and Paul." Kitty Wells, of course, could've stepped on a rainbow by now and God only knew where Charley Pride was at the moment. But at least I knew where Willie Nelson was. He was in his secret compartment at the back of the bus, either sleeping it off, meditating, praying and/or masturbating, plotting his next chess move, plucking his old guitar with the hole in it, or burning sage to keep the bad Indian spirits away. I hadn't particularly liked the look in his eyes when he'd retired the night before and I hadn't heard a sound from the back of the bus since that time. But I knew he had to be alive. He didn't believe in death.

"Now John Wayne was stubborn as hell," Ben Dorsey was saying, "but he couldn't hold a candle up to Willie in the stubborn department. Willie's got stubborn staked out. Now one time I tried to get the Duke and his tequila bottle out of his seven-passenger roadster—"

"I'm sick of hearing about John Wayne," said Gator. "I agree with what Willie says about him: 'He couldn't sing and his horse was never smart.'"

"But if he was here," said Ben, "he'd probably kick your ass."

"No he wouldn't," said Gator. "I'd call L.G."

"No you wouldn't," said L.G., from the bunk where he was supposedly sleeping. "Where the hell's Willie anyway? He's *always* the first one up."

"He's sulking," said Ben, staring balefully at the closed door at the back of the bus.

"How do you know he's not just sleeping?" I suggested, not unreasonably. "Chess has been known to suck almost as much out of a man as a woman."

"Fuck a bunch of chess," said Ben.

"Fuck a bunch of women," said L.G., still from the reclining position.

"The point is," Ben continued, assuming a rather professorial air, "you got to know Willie. Willie's like a kid on Christmas morning. He's got more energy than anyone I ever met."

"Including John Wayne?" shouted L.G.

"Well now," continued Ben, "John Wayne had what you might call a different energy source. He'd drink five bottles of tequila—"

"I'm sick of hearing about John Wayne," said Gator.

There was silence for a while as the bus rolled ever northward through the gray American dawn. The Honeysuckle Rose did not seem to care whether we were bound for a city of our dreams or merely the site of the next gig. In this case, I reflected, it was probably the latter. But when you travelled with Willie Nelson, in the purest sense, of course, that was never really how it was. The next gig would always be the city of his dreams.

Ben Dorsey went back to the small kitchenette that was just across the aisle from Willie's little Ozzie-and-Harriet breakfast nook, which also served as his travelling office and communications center and currently was occupied only by a tiny, forlorn army of chess pieces standing in disarray, the victims of some ill-conceived, mindless military stratagem. In a desultory fashion, Ben brewed a strong pot of coffee. In a desultory fashion, I helped him drink it.

"You think he's sulking," I said, "because he blames himself somehow for the medicine man who went to the happy hunting ground?"

Ben spun around and grapped my wrist so suddenly I almost spilled hot coffee on both of us. Household accident number 436. He had a hell of a grip for a guy who by all rights should've been an executive butt-boy emeritus.

"How'd you find out?" he hissed. "Gator tell you?"

"No," I said. "But Gator got my granny."

"L.G. told you."

"Negative."

"Bobbie's been talking to you about it."

"I'm afraid not."

"I know sure as hell Willie didn't tell you. He's barely got to the point where he'll admit it happened to himself."

Ben released my arm and I used it to pour both of us a fresh head on our coffee. He still seemed in a state of some confusion, but that, quite possibly, was merely the order of the day.

"That only leaves me," Ben said, mainly to himself. "They may be threatenin' to take me away to Coconut University, but they haven't done it yet. And I damn sure don't remember telling you or anybody else about that fucking Indian."

"I didn't hear about it from anybody on the bus. Just rumors 'round the campfire."

"Then what idiot's been flappin' his gums?"

"I can't reveal that in the interest of national security."

"Well, if you know about it, why don't you do something about it? This Indian shit is eating Willie alive. I just feel something real bad is going to happen, and he does, too. You're some kind of big detective up in New York— why don't you start detectin'?"

"Because Willie doesn't need a detective."

"Okay, Mr. Sherlock Holmes. If he doesn't need a detective then what does he need?"

"An exorcist," I said.

Ben Dorsey was not the only person on the bus who was beginning to become mildly agitato. Whatever the nature of the sea change that had occurred within Willie's brain as a result of the incident, it was certainly having a ripple effect upon the crew. But it was not yet the kind of thing that would be noticed by a fan, an audience, or an interviewer like Barbara Walters, who prided herself on asking other human beings if they were happy. Someone had once asked General Charles de Gaulle if he was happy and I still recall his highly insightful answer: "What do you take me for? An idiot?"

Bobbie Nelson wasn't too happy either when I woke her up about an hour later and coaxed her into joining me for coffee at Willie's still empty little table. Bobbie, who'd known Willie longer than any living person on the planet, had become my soulmate some years back when the two of us had driven my mother's little woody convertible out to Palm Springs and back. The car's name was Dusty and it was a talking car, a good vehicle for lonely people, two of which were Bobbie and myself at that time in our lives.

There is something about beautiful, unhappy women that seems to make them particularly soulful as travelling companions. Since life is a journey, not a destination, who rides with you in the Dusty of your dreams can be of lasting, even lingering, importance. Of course, the only woman who might've been more soulful than Bobbie Nelson was Bobby McGee, whom Kris Kristofferson lost on the road in a song. In a vain effort to make up for this

enormous spiritual loss, Kris proceeded in the years immediately following to hose everything that moved in the
state of California. He was quite successful and among his
many conquests, reportedly, was the young Farrah Faw-
cett, about whom Kris was said to have remarked: "Just
enough butt to keep my balls off the bed." But he never
found Bobby McGee again. Nobody else ever found her
again either. Wherever she is, all we can do is hope that
she's happy or, at least, that she never has to do an interview with Barbara Walters.

Now, as I looked across the little table into Bobbie
Nelson's worried eyes, I saw that, indeed, her brother was
always on her mind.

"He was my little brother," she said. "Now he's my
big brother. But I've never seen him quite like this, Kinky.
Through good times and bad, marriages, divorces, deaths
in the family, working so hard all his life and then almost
losing it all to the IRS—through all that I never saw this
look of resignation in his eyes."

"Because of the accident, you think? Come on, Bobbie. It could've happened to a bus full of Shriners or
Japanese tourists. An accident's an accident. Willie knows
that."

Bobbie looked at me thoughtfully. She sipped at her
coffee. When she looked at me again the coffee was the
color of her eyes.

"Fate is fate, Kinky," she said. "Willie knows that, too.
And he seems so resigned to it. I just have this strange
feeling like something terrible's going to happen."

I have learned from experience that certain people
are more in touch with the powers of fate than I often
seem to be. Call it native sensitivity if you like, but when
I'm with this rare kind of individual, against all reason I
tend to trust that person almost more than I trust myself.
Bobbie Nelson was one of these people.

"I'm going to wake Willie up," she said. "He hasn't slept this late since he was a child."

Bobbie put down her coffee cup, got up from the table, and walked down the narrow aisle to Willie's door. She knocked a number of times. There was no response. She tried the door. It was locked.

I was having a hard time defining my role, if, indeed, I had one, within the Willie Nelson Family. Some strange form of photosynthesis was occurring within the Honeysuckle Rose. As an outsider I couldn't quite see it, but I was at the same time enough of an insider to feel it taking place. I felt trapped as the bus hurtled toward Buffalo, as if I were a man in a barrel going over Niagara Falls and having some second thoughts about the project. I thought of Oscar Wilde's insightful comment upon first seeing Niagara Falls: "Second greatest disappointment for American brides."

Then I remembered what I was doing here in the first place. I'd come to travel the open road with the gypsy king, wild and free. To get away from the city of gray, depressed, worn-out souls. But the unfortunate thing about travelling is that you always have to take yourself with you. If you travel with the gypsies, soon you will learn to leave behind the excess baggage of your life. Then one day you find yourself standing with a paper suitcase on the track of time, smoking your old pipe upside down in the rain, like a knight born out of your time, wondering not who you are or how you got there in the first place, but why people have been drinking ginger ale on airplanes for over two thousand years and if women really fake orgasms because they think men care. The next thing you know you're wandering around lost and looking for your locker at Coconut University.

"I've got a spare key," L.G. was saying, as he moved

past me with the speed and agility of a sailor crossing the deck of a sinking ship.

I heard L.G. fumbling with the lock on the door, then I got up from the table and watched the door open. I walked up behind Bobbie and L.G. and gazed into the little room. There was a large mattress of some kind on the floor. It was covered with a bright red-and-black Indian blanket. There was a chest of drawers, one chair, and a little side-table in the room. On the wall over the mattress hung an ornate Navajo dream-catcher. But there didn't seem to be any dreams around to catch.

Willie Nelson wasn't there.

CHAPTER TWENTY

VANISHING ACTS, of course, are nothing new in country music. Hank Williams, whose body and mind were falling apart toward the end of his short career, but whose soul over time has remained surprisingly intact, failed to appear any number of times in his last days. Only a small handful of intrepid promoters, Jack Ruby among them, were willing to touch the boy with a barge pole. George Jones, in more recent years, has practically made a career of not showing up for gigs. Fans came to expect this behavior and, though he often put on a brilliant performance, many were mildly disappointed on those occasions when he actually did show up.

Willie Nelson, however, is a whole other animal. Though he has certainly been capable of highly aberrant behavior that would've made Hank proud, he never quite matched some of George Jones's best moments such as riding a lawnmower into town in order to surreptitiously score alcohol. Yet the one point where Willie had differed markedly from George during his long career is that, unless it is humanly impossible, he always shows up for the gig. Music, to Willie, is, quite simply, the language of his life.

It was unthinkable for Willie to miss a gig, I now reflected, as the Honeysuckle Rose hurtled inexorably toward Buffalo. Willie was so into what he did and what he did was so transcendent that, without missing a beat or adjusting his set, he could give a virtuoso performance at your bar mitzvah, your wedding, or your funeral without knowing, or particularly caring about, the nature of the event. The main thing, the only thing, was that Willie was playing his music. According to Willie, he'd been on automatic pilot for about thirty years now, yet, as far as I could see, in a trivialized, homogenized, sanitized world of chain stores, chain restaurants, and chain people, he was one of the few individuals who was still in tune and in touch. Willie was a life spirit and his guitar was strung with rusty heartstrings that over the years had almost magically brought love into people's lives.

"How in the fuck could the old man have gotten off the bus?" L.G. was saying to nobody in particular.

"I don't know," said Gator, "but I think my pacemaker's redlining. Maybe we should pull off the freeway and check that last truck stop."

"That fucking truck stop is a hundred miles back," said L.G.

"You got a better idea?" said Gator.

"I ain't got any ideas," said L.G. almost despondently. "He ain't never done this before."

"Well," said Gator, "he has now."

I put the linkage together in my mind and I didn't like it at all. The unfortunate accident occurring several months before. The various members of the family I'd spoken to, even those ignorant of the accident itself, nonetheless noticing a worrisome change in Willie. The visit from the Indian who'd given Willie the mysterious package that as yet I hadn't seen. The conversation I'd had with Willie the night before. It all added up to a fairly unpleasant scenario. Either Willie was running from what he perceived to be his demons, or—and this possibility I felt was much more dangerous—he was planning to head them off at the pass on his own. This last approach had not worked very well with General Custer and even in this modern day and age was still not to be recommended.

"If we keep going," I said to Gator, "how long before we get to Buffalo?"

"Two and a half hours," said Gator. "Unless lightning strikes us."

"Which wouldn't surprise me," said L.G.

"And when's the gig?"

"Tomorrow night," said L.G., as he communed morosely with one of the tattoos on his arm.

"Then there's still some time," I said.

"All the time in the world," said L.G.

"That's what I'm worried about," said Bobbie softly.

I turned to Bobbie and saw all the warmth and all the tragedy of a gypsy campfire burning in her eyes. It was apparent that Willie's little disappearing act was not going to be brick and mortar to Bobbie's emotional well-being. She'd already seen the dark side of the moon and now it did not surprise her. It only made the round bright campfires of her eyes glow a little more sadly.

"He'd never go off like this when we're working," she said. "Not without telling me or L.G. or *someone*. The last time he ran away from home without telling me, he was six years old, living in Abbott, Texas, and everybody called him Booger Red."

"Well," I said, glancing briefly at the empty compartment at the back of the bus, "it looks like the little booger's done it again."

CHAPTER TWENTY-ONE

THE DEBATE raged. The bus rolled. Gator was for turning back and checking out the truck stop. L.G. was for going forward, checking into the designated Holiday Inn in Buffalo, and awaiting further developments. Bobbie, who was becoming highly agitato, thought that the best thing to do might be to pray for Willie. I told her that was a good idea. Privately, I didn't put a lot of stock in the power of prayer, but it wasn't a bad way to keep people occupied during traumatic times. If they were praying, at least they'd be less likely to snap their wigs completely and run around shrieking "Am I being rude, mother?" or "Now I have to kill everyone on the elevator." Ben Dorsey's suggestion, over my mild protestations, was that the matter of Willie's disappearance be turned over to the great amateur detective Kinky Friedman, who already happened to be aboard the Honeysuckle Rose. To my dismay, the others seemed to go along with the idea.

"Hold the weddin'," I said. "We really ought to alert the authorities. If there's a possibility of foul play or if—"

"No," shouted L.G. "We're not calling the authorities. Willie gets back, he'll kill me."

"Unless somebody's trying to kill him," I said.

"Who in the world would want to kill Willie?" asked Bobbie.

"I don't *think* anybody's trying to kill Willie," I said. "It's just a possibility that has suggested itself. But conducting this investigation or whatever you want to call it demands more ability and more responsibility than I may currently have in stock. Remember, almost all my experience in crime solving has taken place back in New York. It's a specialized universe. I rely heavily on a small group of good little church workers there called the Village Irregulars. They wouldn't be much help outside of New York City, unfortunately, because most of them don't believe the rest of the world exists."

"Maybe they're right," said Bobbie.

The Honeysuckle Rose hummed along the highway for a mile or more in silence, each occupant caught up in his or her own private thoughts. Mine were particularly tedious and troubling. Of course, when you set out on the road with Willie the Wandering Gypsy, you shouldn't be too surprised if he wanders off somewhere. But that didn't mean it was my duty to God and country music to go out and find him. Or was it? The situation was further complicated, as far as any semblance of an investigation was concerned, by the damnably cosmic natures of both Willie and Bobbie Nelson. A straight answer from either of them was almost out of the question.

Half an hour later, after some more soul-searching, I still hadn't found my soul but had agreed to look into matters a bit with the proviso that if Willie didn't show for the gig the following night, we'd call in the authorities. Bobbie had taken a powder and was lying down in her bunk. L.G. was on the phone to Mark Rothbaum, Willie's manager. I was up front in whatever you call a cockpit on a bus, smoking a cigar, wishing I had room to pace, and going through the motions of interrogating Gator and Ben Dorsey regarding the matter of how Willie had gotten off the bus.

"Cast your mind back to the truck stop, Ben," I said.

"What truck stop?" said Ben.

"What mind?" said Gator.

"There's about a million truck stops back there," said Ben. "How do I know which one you lost him at?"

"*I* lost him?" said Gator.

"Well, *I* sure the hell didn't lose him. I was in the back shinin' shoes when you stopped."

"Is that why I saw you get off the bus?" said Gator.

"It wasn't *me* that got off the bus," shouted Ben. "If it was *me*, how could I be standin' here right now?"

I had to admit there was a certain logic to Ben's argument. Gator, as well, was equally adamant about what he'd observed. If ever so slightly, the fog was beginning to lift. And I didn't think I was going to especially like what I was about to see.

"Ben," I said, "you know that hat with the ear flaps you've been wearing? The one that looks like it belongs to a U-boat commander?"

"Ben probably *thinks* he's a U-boat commander," said Gator, keeping his eyes stonily on the road.

"I wore that hat when I was filming *The Alamo* with John Wayne," said Ben defensively.

"Oh, Jesus," said Gator. "Here we go with John Wayne again."

Indeed, I remembered a photograph of the filming of *The Alamo* that Ben had shown me himself. It was on a wall of the John Wayne Room of the O.S.T. Diner in Bandera, Texas. The photo depicted Wayne and several of the stars of the movie flanked by an ocean of possibly five hundred extras, one of whom, as he'd dutifully pointed out to me, was Ben Dorsey. And, sure enough, Ben had been wearing the U-boat commander's hat in the picture.

"If you don't mind, Ben," I said, "would you check back there and see if you can find your hat and that Willie Nelson and Family coat you were wearing last night."

"My hat? My coat?"

"That's right. Just like what you'd say to a butler in India. Ma hat. Ma coat."

"This is no time for jokes," said Ben, as he scurried toward the back of the bus. Moments later a shriek rang out from somewhere in the background as Gator drove and I stood beside him like a shellshocked soldier staring into what seemed like a boundless theater of gray.

"My hat! My coat!" shouted Ben. "They're gone!"

Gator glance quickly over at me with a worried expression on his weary face. Then, just as quickly, he returned his gaze to the road ahead. I puffed my cigar and stared as the snowflakes silently started to kiss the windshield. For no special reason, a line written by Robert Louis Stevenson crossed the cluttered and dusty desk of my gray-matter department. Stevenson's sentiment was one that any gypsy might take to heart when the night, as it will, becomes too dark, and the road, as it must, becomes too long.

"To travel hopefully," wrote Stevenson, "is a better thing than to arrive."

CHAPTER TWENTY-TWO

THAT EVENING I conducted blower traffic, drank coffee, and smoked cigars in my room. Unlike Brian Wilson, my room was in the Holiday Inn of Greater Buffalo. Like Brian Wilson, I frequently found myself fairly well cookin' on another planet in my frantic efforts to find either hide or hair, and there was plenty of it, of Willie Nelson. The Red Headed Stranger from Blue Balls, Montana, for all the world appeared to be taking Amelia Earhart lessons. As the night wore on and the little room filled up with fragrant cigar smoke, I was becoming increasingly concerned about his health, education, and welfare. Possibly, he'd just needed some time to be alone and think. Possibly, so did I.

Half the people in my little black telephone book were already dead. The other half, many of whom professed mild shock at hearing from me, reported no recent sightings of Willie Nelson, always excluding, of course, occasional television reruns of *The Electric Horseman*. Obviously, he'd taken on the brief role of a Ben Dorsey impersonator to worm his way off the Honeysuckle Rose. Obviously, he wasn't still hanging around the truck stop playing pinball, shopping for belt buckles, and signing autographs for deadhead truckers or whatever you call people who know that wherever the hell they go they'll always be coming back empty. Obviously, he was either laying low or taking things into his own hands. For some reason, neither of these eventualities seemed a very heartening prospect.

By ten o'clock, having coordinated the search-and-rescue operation with L.G., who was staying on the bus manning the cellular phone, the results were not encouraging. L.G. had contacted people mostly inside the Willie Nelson family, including Willie's wife, Annie; Larry Trader; former University of Texas football coach Darryl Royal, Mark Rothbaum, and anyone else he thought Willie might possibly get in touch with. He came up with zip. I tried people a bit more on the periphery of Nelson's superstructure, but they were folks he was close to and conceivably could have called. My list included: Sammy Allred; Bud Shrake, the coauthor of *Harvey Pennick's Little Red Book;* Billy Joe Shaver; Captain Midnite; Little Joe Hernandez; and several other super long shots. I had about as much success as Jim Croce had when he talked to his operator. No one in North America, it would seem, knew of Willie's whereabouts. All I could do was hope he would come home wagging his pigtail behind him.

Not that my little flurry of lake effect blower activity was totally in vain. I did receive several calm assurances as well as hearing a myriad of colorful anecdotes that helped to shed a bit more light on the missing subject. For no matter how well you think you know somebody, there's invariably a world of things about them you find you didn't know, especially if the somebody in question is Willie Nelson. I submit my telephonic intercourse with Sammy Allred that evening as a prime example.

"Good night, nurse!" said Sammy. "He did that to me once, too."

"Yes, but this time there may be some sinister, extenuating circumstances—"

"Hell, in nineteen seventy-four at the Abbott Homecoming there were some sinister extenuating circumstances as well. He gives me a piece of paper on stage with about two hundred performers' names on it and says 'You're in charge. I'll be back in a few minutes.' Well, there were about a zillion people out there in this field chanting 'Leee-onnn! Leeee-ooonnn!'—"

"Were they followers of Leon Trotsky?"

"That would've been more pleasant to deal with. No, they were screaming for Leon Russell, who'd been advertised, but at the last minute, Leon didn't come—"

"Sexually?"

"Didn't attend the concert, shall I say. So I'm up there on stage with the crowd threatening to riot and now a group of local farmers in the next field get out of their pickup trucks with shotguns and claim Willie's concert ain't supposed to be where it is and these other idiots are still screamin' for Leon, who was probably out in California somewhere—"

"So what happened?"

"Eleven hours later Willie came back."

"Did he say anything to you?"

"Yeah. He said: 'Any chance we'll have to fuck our way out of here?' Then he smiled and passed me a joint.

"The next year at his Fourth of July Picnic," Sammy continued, "he proved to me he was truly psychic. It was held at Gonzales or someplace where they hadn't seen rain in seven years and the night before the picnic the sheriff's department was worried that the intense heat might likely cause a riot with all those people crowded out there.

"Willie told them not to worry, that it would rain the next day at six P.M. and cool things off. Six o'clock comes around and damned if it doesn't start pouring, just like Willie'd said, and they have to put a canvas roof over the sound equipment and even that fills up with water until Paul English takes out his gun and shoots a bunch of holes in it and water pours all over the stage. David Allan Coe, who, as you know, once spent several years on death row, was scheduled to be the next performer and I told him 'David, you may get electrocuted yet.' David didn't find it all that humorous."

"Sammy," I said, "let's get back to the current decade for a moment, if we might. Willie may be psychic, but he also may be having a psychic meltdown somewhere out there in the cold, empty American night. Do you think he'll turn up or should we call the authorities?"

"Good night, nurse! Don't call the authorities! He may just appear like a regular Houdini. You know his first wife, Martha, was a friend of mine and a beautiful gal, but she did have a temper. One night in Nashville, back when they were living in a trailer park, he got really drunk and they got into a fight and she chased him through a nearby graveyard with a butcher knife. He got away from her and later she found him passed out in the trailer. So Martha sewed him up in the bedsheet, whacked the hell out of him with a broomhandle, took the kids, and left him there. If he could survive that night, hell, he can survive anything. Lord Almighty, she had a temper. Martha was an Indian, you know."

I'd been only rather amusedly half-listening to this point, but now Sammy's last sentence struck me like a tomahawk in the forehead.

"Jay-zuz Christ!" I said. "I'd forgotten that. She stepped on a rainbow, didn't she?"

"Yes," said Sammy. "She went to the happy hunting ground years ago. Whatever Willie's current problems are, at least we know Martha's got nothing to do with them."

"I wouldn't be too sure," I said.

After talking with Sammy, I felt there was at least a decent chance that Willie would mysteriously show up in time for the gig the following night. There was also the chance that something *really* weird was going on here. L.G. and I had decided to take a fairly relaxed approach with our blower campaign, so as not to create a panic and make everybody highly agitato even if we were beginning to feel that way ourselves. We were also keenly aware that, if Willie indeed returned and found out what we'd been doing, he might, like Jesus, very conceivably be extremely pissed.

By midnight, I was starting to run out of charm myself. I didn't want to get my bowels in a twist over this thing. If Willie returned in time for the gig the next night, it'd all be no big deal. It'd just mean that I'd spent a rather hideous evening calling people from the Holiday Inn of Greater Buffalo while Willie Nelson had once again travelled somewhere through the looking glass of my bathroom mirror back on Vandam Street, which, at the moment, seemed a far more pleasant locus.

If Willie Nelson failed to return, the situation could get very unpleasant indeed. Should I put out an APB on Shotgun Willie? Should I attempt to suck, fuck, or cajole Rambam into the investigation? Should I reach out to my Indian friend Robby Romero or Willie's buddy Dennis Alley and try to pass a peace pipe around the planet before it was too late? And what about interrogating Just Bill again or searching for the small buckskin package that L.G. was now reporting he couldn't find in Willie's little room at the back of the bus?

I had a lot of executive decisions to make, I reflected grimly, as I walked down the empty hotel corridors at two in the morning, an undaunted pilgrim looking for a Dr. Pecker machine and a bucket of ice. This was especially true for a guy who'd left the big city to run off with the gypsies. Why couldn't my problem be simple like the problem that had befallen my friend Dylan Ferrero, the former road manager for the Texas Jewboys? Dylan had recently pulled a muscle in his back, apparently while wiping his ass.

Such were my bright and dark and multifaceted reflections as I walked through the valley of the shadow of ennui with a Dr. Pecker can in one hand and a bucket of ice in the other, smoking a Montecristo No. 2 cigar and thinking of myself as a human locomotive puffing along in the pursuit of crime. I was planning to shovel on a bit more coal when I got back to my room by cracking open a large bottle of Jameson Irish Whiskey and backing it up with a little red caboose of Dr. Pecker. I never got that far, however.

I was just rounding the bend in the corridor when I heard what sounded like a Panzer tank backfiring in the parking lot. The noise occurred just as I was passing the Niagara Suite, which, I'd noted on the room chart L.G. had provided, was registered in the name of one Larry Jackson.

Seconds after the backfire sound came the unmistakable dull thud of a human body falling to the carpet on the floor of a Holiday Inn hotel room in Buffalo, New York. This was followed, inevitably, by the sound of silence, like the silence after the parade has passed, the ball game has ended, the war is over, the last human soldier having fallen on the beach on a perfect day for banana fish. Total silence. Nature-bats-last silence.

The door to the Niagara Suite was open, but the only roar I heard was the blood rushing to my brain as I set down my Dr. Pecker and bucket of ice and stepped inside. The suite was big and dark and I decided to keep it that way. The first thing I saw once my eyes adjusted to the darkness was the bullet hole in the window with little spidery lines extending out from it in all directions. The second thing I saw, lost in the shadows of the far side of the room, was the dim outline of a body on the floor.

I knew it wasn't Larry Jackson. Larry Jackson didn't exist. Larry Jackson was the name used by Willie Nelson so people wouldn't disturb him when he stayed in hotels.

Apparently, somebody had.

CHAPTER TWENTY-THREE

THE DEAD BODY on the floor of the Niagara Suite, I noticed with great relief, did not appear to belong to Willie Nelson. It seemed too long and thin and ragged. It was some moments later, with no little shock, that I noticed that the body did not appear to even be dead. It was lying on its face and only as I was turning the body over in the darkness did I realize the corpse was not a corpse. A hand came out of the blackness and grabbed my wrist. I glanced around in a mild panic only to observe that no one else was in the room but my body and the body. The hand obviously was attached to the body and the desperate, talonlike grip felt vaguely familiar. It had now become patently clear that the unfortunate victim was either Ben Dorsey or the scarecrow from *The Wizard of Oz*.

I crawled over to the window like a paranoid spider, reached up and closed the curtains, then I quickly hit the lights and two-stepped it over to the telephone to order one meat wagon to go. Ben was the kind of guy who looked half dead half the time even when he was moving around in a vertical position. When he was lying on the floor in a puddle of blood, it was somewhat harder to determine his precise mortal status from moment to moment.

"Ben," I said, kneeling beside him, "just hang in there. Help is on the way."

"I can hear the cavalry, Duke," said Ben, his eyelids fluttering. "They're comin' to save us."

"This is Kinky, Ben. You're here at the Holiday Inn. You've been shot, but you're going to be fine."

"I'm with you, Duke. But wait a minute! What's that I'm hearin'? Is it the cavalry comin' or is it the angels?"

"It's neither one of them, Ben. Somebody's using the ice machine out in the hall."

The bullet appeared to have lodged in the area of Dorsey's right shoulder. I wasn't a doctor, but I could think of worse places to catch a little lead. If I had been a doctor, no doubt I wouldn't have been here making a hotel call. I'd've been chasing a nurse around the operating table while my wife was home hosing the boy who cleans the pool. But I was here, getting blood on my hands and britches, wondering if some idiot with a deer rifle was currently studying my silhouette from the woods beyond the parking lot, and trying to calm a severely injured elderly man who believed he was conversing with John Wayne.

"What were you doing in here in the first place, Ben?" I said, in an effort to keep him talking and ward off possible shock.

"You called me, Duke. I had to get through. Had to bring you the message from General Custer."

The whole experience was now taking on a strange, almost cinematic feel. If I'd mistaken Ben for Willie, very possibly someone else had, too. I didn't think Dorsey was dying. I'd managed to stop most of the blood flow with a few well-placed hotel towels. But maybe the angels were coming and I didn't know it. Possibly Ben was already slipping into shock, picking up on my cowboy hat, and, quite naturally under the circumstances, thinking I was John Wayne. In this kind of sorry situation, in which the victim is teetering tenuously upon the dull razor blade of mortality, John Wayne was, no doubt, as worthy a companion to have around as any. Jesus was always another good possibility, of course, but Ben didn't seem to be seeing Him tonight. Probably He was working late in the city.

"Well," I said, ratcheting up my best bedside manner, "what does Custer want from me this time?"

"Hell," said Ben, "I don't know. He just gave it to me. Said not to open it. Said to bring it to you pronto. Said it's top secret."

"You've done good work, Ben. Now where's the message?"

"Under the bed."

When you operate on a mind-set of no surprises there's very little that tends to surprise you. So it was that hundreds of people continued to sleep in their sanitized cubicles all around us and desk clerks proceeded with the process of checking people in and checking people out and a conversation straight out of a mental ward was taking place in the Niagara Suite between myself and a person who might really be checking out. I thought more than once about making a run to my own room for the bottle of Jameson, but I didn't want to leave Ben alone. At the moment, I felt certain that both of us could've used a shot, always precluding, of course, the one that Dorsey had already received.

"Did you see who shot you, Ben?"

"It was the Indians, Duke. They got me."

At this point, Ben placed his hand dramatically over his heart. Despite his injury, he certainly seemed to be enjoying our little conversation a hell of a lot more than I was. I was still waiting for the cavalry.

"They didn't get you, Ben. You're going to be fine." If the paramedics ever show up, I thought.

"Ain't you gonna read it, Duke?" said Ben, his hand

still over his heart even though he'd been shot in the right shoulder, his eyes boring into mine like a death scene in *Duel in the Sun*.

"Read what?"

"The message from Custer, of course!"

"Okay," I said distractedly. "Where the hell is it?"

"It's under the fucking bed, Duke. You been drinkin' again, haven't you?"

"No, I haven't been, Ben, but I'd like to be."

To humor Dorsey, I lifted up the bedspread and was peering into the murkiness under the bed when the paramedics and hotel management all came thundering into the room pretty much like, well, a herd of cavalry. Incredibly, I saw something under the bed. It was a small parcel wrapped in what appeared to be buckskin. I grabbed it, tucked it under my shirt, and got out of the way for the paramedics.

I also got out of the way for the cops, who, I now observed from the doorway, were rapidly coming down the hall. Letting the ice bucket and Dr. Pecker breath a while in the corridor, I headed like a heat-seeking missile for the sanctuary of my room so I could explode in private. I locked and chained the door, put the little buckskin package on the coffee table, and extracted the bottle of Jameson from my suitcase.

Dispensing with the cellophane-wrapped plastic glasses in the dumper, I decided to drink the most hygienic way of all, right from the bottle. Just like the Old West, I thought, as I poured a posttraumatic shot down my neck. I felt like Niagara Falls had just attacked my uvula, but it seemed to give the rest of me a nice little radioactive glow.

I'd set fire to a fresh cigar and was considering whether to open the parcel or whether to open my mouth and pour down another round of Jameson when the phone rang. I walked over and collared the blower. It was L.G. Loud music was playing in the background. I started to tell him about Ben, but I didn't get around to it.

"Willie's back," he said.

CHAPTER TWENTY-FOUR

It'd been a long, eventful night and as long, eventful nights have a way of doing, it wasn't about to let go of itself until morning. By the time I got out to the back parking lot of the Holiday Inn to talk to Willie, the Honeysuckle Rose was gone. Mickey Raphael and Just Bill were conversing together under a cute little Holiday Inn streetlamp when I walked up. They stopped abruptly when they saw me.

"Where the hell did they go?" I said.

"Gator said they're going to the hospital," said Mickey. "I heard Ben got sick."

"That's one way of putting it," I said.

"What happened to him?" asked Just Bill, a trifle uneasily.

"It's a little unpleasant," I said, stalling for time. It wasn't going to be a secret for long, I figured, so I might as well spit it.

"Care to share it with the rest of the class?" said Mickey.

"Somebody shot him."

"Goddamn," said Just Bill. "Mugger or jealous husband?"

"Neither," I said.

"Jesus Christ," said Mickey, "I've felt like shooting Ben many times myself, but who would actually do it?"

"He claims the Indians got him," I said.

Mickey's face looked totally mystified, but Just Bill merely stared at me and began nodding his head slowly, like a man reading smoke signals in the distance.

In the wake of the shooting, police presence was beginning to pick up in the parking lot. I'd cooperate if I had to, but I wasn't very confident about what I could deliver. My mind was rather busy at the moment ciphering smoke signals myself. Where had Willie gone and why? Why had he returned so conveniently close to the time Ben had been shot? And did the shooter, who, on the face of things had mistaken Ben for Willie, even know of Willie's absence from the scene? This was a study in scarlet all right, but even more so than the one to which Conan Doyle had alluded. The scarlet represented not only "the scarlet thread of murder running through the colorless skein of life," but also the ubiquitous involvement of the American Indian in this troublesome matter.

Partly to avoid running prematurely into the police and partly because I wanted to be alone to think, in the manner of Henry David Thoreau, or Robert Frost, or Emily Dickinson, I took a little walk in the woods. The cops, no doubt, would be talking to Ben and, eventually, myself, and Willie, too, for that matter. They might even ask Willie to sign some autographs or pose for some photographs with them. Right now they seemed to be focusing a rather hivelike activity on the parking area just adjacent to the wing of the motel that housed the infamous Niagara Suite. Walking deeper into the woods, I could see cop cars with searchlights and men on foot with flashlights hoping to find a trace of the assailant. But Ben Dorsey's Indian, I was very much afraid, had vanished from the land, not unlike his ancient culture and his fathers before him, leaving nothing for the police to find other than a heap of towns and cities that bore his name, along with a few baseball and football teams, and about a million rivers running relentlessly into somebody else's shining sea.

Maybe it had been Ben's dramatic gesture toward the horizon that unconsciously caused me to believe the bullet had come from a great distance, certainly farther than the parking area. The Indians had been remarkable marksmen, often aligning three arrows as a fragile tripod and felling game an incredible distance away. Historically, the Indians called this technique "the long shot." I called it a long shot, too.

I was weaving my way through the shivering timbers at about half past a buffalo's ass when I came to a small clearing. My mind was clearing a bit as well and darting through it like little deer in the forest were the surgical questions I soon planned to put to Willie Nelson. Every time I almost thought I had a handle on this thing I'd somehow seemed to lose my grip. Now, I thought, at least I knew what had to be done.

I was standing in the clearing in the silvery moonlight when I looked down and noticed something silvery on the frozen forest floor at my feet. It was a shell casing a little over an inch long. I realized at once that any local bullethead could've fired the bullet's head into the peaceful little head of some harmless forest creature. That was the way many people chose to spend what little time they had on the planet. Others, of course, chose to spend their time freezing their ass off in the middle of the night walking around picking up the shell casings.

I picked up the shell casing and put it in the pocket of my blue overcoat that looked like a hand-me-down from Oliver Twist. When I stood up again and looked in the direction of the Holiday Inn, an insect seemed to run up my spine. Though thick woods surrounded the hotel, abutting almost directly upon the parking lot's edge and continuing well past the little clearing, the precise point where I stood gave way to a direct, unimpeded view of the Niagara Suite.

CHAPTER TWENTY-FIVE

"GIVE ME an eye-opener, honey," said Willie Nelson to his daughter, Lana. It was four o'clock in the morning and Willie was sitting across from me on the bus appearing for all the world like a cheerful little leprechaun.

"Comin' right up, Daddy," said Lana, as if she were a little girl bringing her father orange juice at the suburban breakfast table before he went to work in the morning.

"Bring Kinky an eye-opener, too," said Willie. "He looks like he needs one."

"Not really," I said. "My eyes always look like two piss-holes in the snow."

Lana drew two glasses of water from the little sink in the kitchen of the bus. Then she began to meticulously pour a good number of drops of Tabasco sauce into each glass. She stopped when the water took on an appearance not dissimilar to that of the water in the shower scene in *Psycho*. She brought the two eye-openers over to the little table.

"Hope you enjoy our beverage service, Mr. Fried-man," she said.

Lana Nelson had her father's eyes. After all the things they had seen, I reflected, they still appeared hopeful. There were four marriages in those eyes, matching Willie's four marriages, but nobody was really counting. As Lana herself once observed: "I've got miles and miles of exes." As Allen Ginsberg once observed: "The apple never falls far from the tree, even when the tree has fallen down." The tree, indeed, had almost fallen down in Nashville when Willie's personal and professional life had seemed to hit rock bottom at precisely the same time. He'd been out all night writing songs with Hank Cochran. In the early hours of the morning the last song they'd written was called "What Can You Do to Me Now?" Willie went home afterward and found that his house had burned down. Lana was just a young girl then, but if you look closely you can see that some of the embers still seem to be smoldering in her eyes.

Like Willie and Bobbie, she was a fighter who never gave up. When one of her exes had beaten up on her, then had gone into rehab, she'd held out some hope for him. Willie had commented at the time that rehab was "where they go to rest up before they come back at us again." In this instance, it was true, because the soon-to-be-ex-husband came back and, quite unintentionally, provided Lana with one of the greatest lines of her life. After he'd returned and had started to whip up on her again, she finally had had enough and pushed the guy down a flight of stairs.

"How's that for a twelve-step program?" she'd asked him.

"To your health," said Willie, lifting his glass in a toast. "And to Ben's health."

"And to your health," I added.

Ben's health, as I had learned when I'd first entered the bus, had never really been in question. The injury, as I had surmised, had not been life-threatening, and the doctors were keeping him in the hospital one night only for observation. They said his body was as strong as a horse's. His mind, of course, was another matter, but that would require another kind of doctor, preferably the kind with a rather advanced degree from Coconut University.

"At least," said Willie, after knocking back the eye-opener, "Ben seems to now realize that you're not John Wayne. He's still sticking to his story about getting shot by the Indians, however."

"Does that surprise you?" I said. What mildly surprised me was that I could speak at all after drinking my eye-opener. On the positive side, even at four in the morning, it did tend to make you leap sideways.

"Nothing Ben could ever say would surprise me," said Willie.

"You've got a point there," I said. "But forgetting John Wayne and the Alamo for the moment, it's this nagging little scarlet thread that's still troubling me. The tour bus T-bones an Indian. Some time later a young Native American gentleman shows up with a buckskin-wrapped package of grief and hands it to you. You bug out for the dugout, as you told me earlier, 'to play golf in a warmer climate,' and while you're gone, the buckskin package disappears. Then it turns up again in the Niagara Suite of the hotel, a room registered to you under the name Larry Jackson, where Ben has gone in the belief he's carrying the parcel on orders from General Custer to be delivered to John Wayne. In real life, of course, Ben used to work for John Wayne. In real life, he now works for you. Then something happens that's indisputably real life: Ben gets shot. He claims he was shot by an Indian. He tells me the buckskin parcel is under the bed. I reach under and get it and take it to my room and carefully peruse the contents. I bring it back to you. You put it on this little table between us. And now we're both sitting here like Faron Young at four o'clock in the morning staring at the damn thing, both of us inextricably bound by that nagging little scarlet thread, both of us wondering just exactly what the hell is going to happen next."

It was my longest speech to date on the subject, but

Willie was not only a great performer, he was also a great audience. He not only absorbed every word but also picked up on the nuances, doubts, and implications of what I'd said. He looked at me with the eyes of a snake charmer.

"You got any ideas?" he said.

"I left my crystal balls in my other trousers," I said. "But I do have one suggestion."

"What's that?" said Willie, as he calmly lit up a joint about as large as the Holland Tunnel.

"It may be almost time to circle the buses," I said.

It was a bloody mary morning by the time I managed to dart, like a daring little hummingbird, away from the Honeysuckle Rose and into a strange and dangerous dawn. At Willie's request, I carried with me the ubiquitous, neatly wrapped buckskin albatross, to which more evil seemed to be accruing with every moment I held it in my hands. I now had a formal understanding with Willie that I would officially take up this unusual investigation and do my damnedest to determine who or what was behind this unpleasant situation. A formal deal with Willie, of course, is a handshake and a smile, but it was good enough for me and, no doubt, good enough for Bobby McGee wherever the hell she was.

The way I now saw things, there was a tiny bit of housekeeping still to be done and then it'd be time to shuffle off from Buffalo and head back to little ol' New York for a brief sabbatical from the road. I wanted to refocus things a tad. I wanted to stand back a bit, get an overview, and study the problem as one might stop at a roadside park to peacefully peruse a road map to hell. I wanted to have a powwow with Rambam, my chief technical consultant in all criminal matters. And, what the hell, I also wanted to see the cat.

So it was that twenty-four hours later I was aboard an aircraft on my way from Buffalo to JFK. It didn't really feel like I was coming home, however. For one thing, I had a very vague, almost evanescent, concept of home. For another, leaving the road is not the kind of thing that is quickly or easily done. Sometimes it takes a lifetime. Sometimes it takes longer. Sometimes the road is in the sky.

PART THREE

GOD

THROW DOWN the fuckin' puppet head," shouted Rambam, his irritation level somewhat elevated by the steady frozen drizzle cascading relentlessly onto the sidewalk below.

The cat and I watched the spectacle from the kitchen window of my fourth-floor loft. I was wearing my old Robert Louis Stevenson purple bathrobe, drinking a cup of hot, bitter espresso, and smoking part two of an ancient Cuban cigar I'd resurrected from my large, Texas-shaped ashtray. I had to admit it felt good to be back in New York.

Just for fun I feigned a momentary lack of understanding in regard to the transparently obvious intentions of our vehemently vexed visitor below on Vandam Street.

"What do you think the crazy man wants?" I said to the cat.

The cat, of course, said nothing. She did, however, take another hard look at Rambam's antics down in the street. He was stomping like a Cossack with St. Vitus' dance. He was shrieking like a wounded faggot. He was waving his arms like a goddamn Shostakovich. The cat looked at me doubtfully.

"There's something familiar about the voice," I said.

The cat said nothing.

"Throw down that fuckin' puppet head," shouted Rambam in a rage.

Fun is fun, I thought, but you don't want to push a

guy like Rambam too far. For one thing, I was going to need his help if I was ever going to get to the bottom of this Willie Nelson caper. For another, I didn't want to be walking down the street one day and suddenly find out that my cowboy hat had exploded.

With all attendant haste I walked over to the refrigerator, removed the little black smiling puppet head, raised the window a bit, and tossed that beloved object out into the cold, uncaring New York City afternoon. The wind had picked up a bit, apparently, for the gaily-colored parachute carried the puppet head on a trajectory well over Rambam's head. Not to be thwarted, with an almost superhuman effort, Rambam launched himself into the street, narrowly missing being garroted by a slow-moving garbage truck rendezvousing with a nearby Dumpster, and performed a circus catch.

"Allah be praised," I said to the cat, as I closed the window.

The cat, who, in a former life was a charismatic Episcopalian, did not respond favorably to my rather facetious fundamentalist fervor. Instead, she merely continued to stare with a measure of cynical feline displeasure at Rambam, who was not responding particularly favorably to the situation either. Then, as we watched in horror, Rambam jerked the key out of the little puppet head's smiling mouth and held it high over his head. With his other hand he viciously spiked the little puppet head onto the frozen sidewalk.

"Jesus Christ!" I shouted, at last drawing a strong reaction from the cat, who jumped down from the windowsill, rolled over several times on the floor, and began speaking in tongues.

A short while later, as the rain continued to fall upon all the arkless Noahs in the street, the puppet head was back on top of the refrigerator smiling stoically, the cat was curled up asleep under her private heat lamp on my desk, and Rambam and I were leisurely sipping espresso at the kitchen table as I related to him my recent road trip, mile by mile. Telling someone about an experience is never quite the same as being there, even if, at times, you wish you hadn't been. There were moments when I felt Rambam was absorbing the ambience so well that it almost seemed we were back on the bus together with Willie and his band of gypsies. There were other moments when Rambam didn't seem to be riding with me at all, and I felt like Marco Polo trying to introduce the noodle to a crowd of irritated Italians.

Three hours, six espressos, four cigars, and half a bottle of Jameson later, it was growing very dark outside, but inside, a new and more clearly focused light was beginning to shine upon what was surely a broad and murky landscape. The cat was now wide awake and I noticed, with no little degree of relief, that Rambam's eyes were almost matching her own in intensity. Instead of making the rather blunt rejoinder, "What's your point?", he was now emitting mildly more helpful ejaculations such as, "You got to be kidding," and, "This is fucking crazy." I was greatly encouraged.

Rambam's "hard-boiled computer" approach and his legal and sometimes extralegal expertise had quite often been invaluable at those times when an investigation had somehow managed to wander out where the buses don't run. I was hoping this general dictum would, as well, apply to Willie Nelson's tour bus.

I killed another shot of Jameson and watched as Rambam made a few small notes to himself in his little criminal investigator's notebook. This was a good sign indeed. As I looked at my sometimes surly, sometimes charming friend, I recalled with grudging gratitude his help with a case McGovern had written about and cryptically entitled *The*

Love Song of J. Edgar Hoover. It had involved a dead Chicago mobster who'd once been Al Capone's chef and, after his death, had appeared to make threatening phone calls to McGovern. The investigation had turned on Rambam's hard-boiled computer research, during which he'd discovered that a man I'd been pursuing for three months did not exist.

"Well, Travis McGee," said Rambam, leaning back comfortably in his chair, "you know what you've got to do now."

"I do?" I said, looking questioningly at the cat for help and, as usually occurs when petitioners appeal to cats, getting no reaction at all.

"You've given me lots of background on Willie," said Rambam, referring to his notes. "Let's see. You've described him as a child picking cotton in a field in some little town in Texas—"

"Abbott, Texas," I said.

"Fuckhead, Texas," said Rambam. "It doesn't matter. He's telling you a story about him as a kid seeing big cars drive by on the highway with their windows rolled up in the middle of the summertime and thinking that was where he wanted to be instead of the cotton fields. It's kind of poignant that that was his idea of success at that stage of his life but it also shows that even back then he was into the notion of wealth and power."

"Can you pass the cocaine, Dr. Freud?"

"The point is I don't entirely buy his cosmic, fatalistic, Zen approach to life. The fact that he doesn't seem terribly excited about finding out who may be trying to kill him—"

"Willie doesn't get terribly excited about anything."

"Neither do I," said Rambam. "Unless somebody touches my car. Then there's the impression he gave you that he doesn't believe in death, yet he takes this very meticulous regimen for his health—"

"It's for energy. I'm taking it myself now."

"You're kidding? Let's see. You're taking two bee pollen tablets every day?"

"That's correct."

"An unspecified but incredibly large number of chlorella pills made from some kind of seaweed?"

"That's correct."

"And each day you drink a few swigs—just like your mentor—of—let me see—raw, unfiltered apple cider vinegar?"

"That's correct. Did anybody ever tell you you'd make a pretty fair stenographer?"

"Did anybody ever tell you you'd make a pretty fair total fucking idiot? How do you know what this stuff could do to you? This could just be what Willie takes to keep his dick hard."

"So that's why I've been walking around with a nine-foot-long monstro-erection for the past three months."

"And I thought that was your foot under the table."

"So are you going to help with this or not?" I said, suddenly tired of the bantering and anxious to have Rambam on the case with me.

"That depends," said Rambam, folding up his little notebook and studying me carefully.

"Depends on what?" I said.

"Depends on whether that was your foot under the table," said Rambam.

CHAPTER TWENTY-SEVEN

THE RAIN continued to fall even as the dream-woven Indian blanket of childhood night fell upon the city. The level of the bottle of Jameson fell, too. Soon the Jameson was gone, but Rambam, the cat, and myself were still there, bonded mortally together by rain, ennui, and circumstance, like desperate, disparate characters who wander lost for a lifetime, then find each other at last in the middle of a forgotten French novel.

"Surely it's occurred to you by this time," said Rambam, "that all this crazy business with the Indians would make a very convenient cover for anyone who really wanted to harm Willie Nelson."

"To paraphrase Bobbie Nelson," I said, " 'Who in the world would want to harm Willie Nelson?' "

"Me," said Rambam, "if I have to hear him sing 'Mamas Don't Let Your Babies Grow Up To Be Jewboys' again."

"But you couldn't have been the guy who mistakenly shot Ben Dorsey. You were jumping with the Sri Lankan Army Paratroopers at the time."

"The Royal Thai Paratroopers. And what makes you so sure somebody wasn't actually gunning for Ben Dorsey?"

"Because Ben's always mistaken for Willie. Willie often uses this to his benefit. He told me that when he used to get off the bus first in front of a crowd of fans he

would sometimes hear somebody say: 'God, he looks old.'
So he started letting Ben get off the bus first. When people
saw Ben they'd say 'God, he looks old.' Willie'd wait a few
moments, then he'd get off the bus and people would say:
'God, Willie looks great.' "

"That's good," said Rambam, laughing to himself.
"Very clever. Don't you think Willie's clever enough to
know a lot more about this business than he's told you?"

"It's possible."

"More than possible. What if he knows or suspects
who's behind this and doesn't want to tell you? What if he
thinks it's somebody close to him? Maybe someone who
works for him? As you've said, practically all of them have
served time."

"I don't think so," I said. "Willie's family is loyal to
him unto death."

"Which is where this investigation might just lead if
you're wrong."

It was a sobering thought, all right. And I needed a
sobering thought after helping kill almost a whole bottle
of Jameson. I lit a cigar for ballast and walked over to
the espresso machine, which was now busily humming a
close approximation of "Blow High, Blow Low," the
whaling song from *Carousel*. It was one of the best
songs in the show but, alas, it didn't make the movie. I
drew two cups of strong, hot, bitter espresso to sort of
keep a handle on the Jameson buzz. I brought the cups
back to the table, gave one to Rambam, and sat down
across from him again. Now if we could just get a handle
on this investigation.

"I don't think Willie's people could be involved in
anything that would consciously hurt him," I said. "There's
a certain morality in the criminal mind that doesn't often
manifest itself in the general population."

"You're probably right," said Rambam. "It sounds like

the people around him would go through hell for him. Take great personal risks for the man. That sort of thing. Like the dope-sniffing dog story you told earlier."

Rambam was referring to the incident early on in the tour when feds had stopped the bus after a show in McAllen, Texas, at three o'clock in the morning. Ben had desperately tried to hide the marijuana, but it was a task roughly comparable to hiding the sand at Waikiki. Willie, L.G., Gator, Bobbie, Lana, Ben, and myself had been ordered off the bus. We stood around for a while in a freezing federal cop shop with a sad Mexican woman and two ragged, beautiful children watching the extremely clean-cut, impossibly young federal agents talking over the situation.

"They look almost too young to know who Willie Nelson is," I'd commented to Gator.

"*Everyone* knows who Willie Nelson is," he'd said.

This, of course, presented another problem. Many bureaucratic minds, like those in the IRS and law enforcement in general, tend to lack some of the morals and imagination that seemed to thrive in the outlaw community. Many a constipated, humorless upholder of the law might recognize an icon like Willie Nelson and see in him the prize catch of an otherwise pathetic career. When Willie was nailed for possession of pot while sleeping it off in his pickup on the side of the highway near Waco, an interesting situation had occurred. There'd been an older cop and a younger cop involved in the incident. The older cop was all for letting the country music legend go. It was the younger cop who insisted upon pushing the envelope. The envelope in this case, unfortunately, contained several Willie-sized joints of marijuana. The older cop was still, reportedly, in favor of letting him off the hook. It was the younger officer who was out for blood. It was the younger one who'd insisted upon bringing him in and making the arrest to subsequent national headlines.

Like I said, the federal agents near McAllen looked impossibly young. Maybe they'd known who Willie Nelson was, but it was a cinch they'd never heard of Hank Williams, Anne Frank, Wavy Gravy, Adlai Stevenson, Father Damien, Ira Hayes, Breaker Morant, or Emily Dickinson. If they had, they probably would've busted them, too. Just following orders.

It was at about this point that another young agent had walked over leading an incredibly eager, alert-looking, specially trained, no-nonsense German shepherd. The sad eyes of the Mexican woman along with all the rest of our bloodshot eyes looked on as the fed opened the door of the Honeysuckle Rose and walked inside with the dog. We could see the head of the young officer moving slowly back and forth along the whole length of the bus. Over the years the amount of weed smoked aboard the Honeysuckle Rose had so heavily permeated those environs that even a sniff of that flower would make you high enough to sing castrato in the Vienna Boys Choir. The Mexican woman looked over at us sympathetically.

We stood around for about forty years in the South Texas desert and then—lo and behold!—a miracle had occurred. The young fed and the German shepherd were walking away and another young fed was motioning us back on the bus and waving us on our way.

"Jesus Christ," I'd said. "What the hell could've happened?"

"Maybe the dog was a Willie fan," Lana had suggested.

"Maybe it was a Kinky fan," Willie had said, with a smile.

"Or maybe," Bobbie had murmured, "it had a sinus condition."

"I feel sure," I said to Rambam now as I puffed the cigar and smiled ruefully at the memory, "that we can cross the whole Willie Nelson Family off the list."

"Which brings us to the obvious point we should've started from. What about Willie's *earlier* families? Specifically, his ex-wives. I'd bet on one of them being behind all this."

Husbands and wives, I thought, reflecting back on the old Roger Miller song of that title. It made all the sense in the world.

"How many ex-wives does Willie have?" Rambam asked.

I puffed on the cigar a bit and took another slurp of espresso.

"About ninety-seven," I said.

At this point the meeting seemed upon the verge of adjournment. Rambam stood up and performed what appeared to be an attenuated version of a Burmese Army stretching exercise. I walked over to the desk to bring to his attention what little evidence I had brought back from the road. And just at that moment, the lesbian dance class suddenly kicked into high gear with various thuddings, sinuous sliding sounds, and just plain pounding noises raining down mercilessly upon the ceiling of the loft. There was only one positive thought I now held in regard to Winnie Katz's lesbian dance classes: none of them was ever likely to become one of Willie Nelson's wives.

"Here's a little show-and-tell," I said, as I placed the shell casing I'd found in the woods and the mysterious buckskin package in Rambam's hands, thereby slowing his progress to the door. He took the shell casing over to the desk and examined it under the lamp, thus causing a mild display of irritation on the part of the cat, who had now gone back to sleep under her heat lamp.

"Found it in a little forest clearing just across the way

from where Ben Dorsey was shot. The clearing is in a direct line with the Niagara Suite that I told you about."

"Holy shit," said Rambam, holding the little silver casing up to the light.

"What is it?"

"Haven't seen one like this in a while."

"What is it?"

"I don't know," said Rambam, "but it looks like it's been hanging around in Don Knott's pocket for about thirty-five years."

"You mean it's old?"

"The kind of thing the sheriff of Tombstone might've worn on his belt. If you don't mind, I'll take it with me and have it checked out."

"What about this mysterious buckskin package the Indian gave Willie in Florida?"

"Can't say," said Rambam, studying the contents. "That'll have to be your department. I'll jump on the ninety-seven ex-wives and you deal with the Indians."

"Why don't you want to help me with the Indians?"

"Let's just say," said Rambam, as he headed for the door, "that I have some reservations."

CHAPTER TWENTY-EIGHT

IN THE EARLY fifties, when I was a child, I spat as a child, I shat as a child, and I wore a funny little pointed birthday hat as a child. I knew what every little kid knows about Indians, which, in a purely spiritual sense, can often be considerable, and of course absolutely nothing about ex-wives. When I grew up and was finally released from the Bandera Home for the Bewildered for rhyming words too frequently, I knew a little more about Indians and still absolutely nothing about ex-wives except what Alden Shuman had once told me: "They'll stick with you through thick."

As far as Indians go, which is usually a good bit farther than ex-wives, I've collected about a million arrowheads over the years and made frequent visits to the Frontier Times Museum in Bandera, which is just down the street from the Bandera Home for the Bewildered. As well as countless Indian artifacts, the museum features a real shrunken head, a two-headed goat, a "shoe of a Negress" involved in a 1927 hit-and-run accident, and many other weird and arcane objects that delighted me as a child and, because of a rather unfortunate state of arrested development, continue to hold the same fascination for me now.

Children, it has always seemed to me, have a greater inherent understanding of many things than adults. As they grow up, this native sensitivity is smothered, buried,

and destroyed, like someone pouring concrete over cob-
blestones, and finally replaced by what we call knowledge.
Knowledge, according to Albert Einstein, who spent a lot
of time, incidentally, living with the Indians when he
wasn't busy forgetting his bicycle in Princeton, New Jersey, is a vastly inferior commodity when compared with
imagination. Imagination, of course, is the money of childhood. This is why it is no surprise that little children have
a better understanding of Indians, nature, death, God,
animals, the universe, and some truly hard to grasp con-
cepts like the Catholic Church, than most adults.

Now, with the eyes of a child, I lit my first cigar of
the morning and focused softly on everything that wasn't
there. I'd survived half a fucking century on this primitive
planet where the pecking of poison parakeets in the
Northern Territories of Australia was the very least of our
worries. I cast my mind back to when I was seven years
old, sitting like Otis Redding on the dock at the deep
water at Echo Hill Ranch in the Texas summertime. It was
there and then that a rather seminal experience occurred
in my young life, a small thing actually, but as Raymond
Chandler often observed in his final stages of alcoholism:
"Tiny steps for tiny feet." It was the first time I'd ever seen
a man's testicle, unknowingly suspended, almost like a Bla-
kean symbol, outside the lining of his fifties-style bathing
suit.

The man was named Danny Rosenthal, a nice man
with a mustache and a cheery smile, who probably had
had his own problems by then, but, of course, as a child,
these were not known to me. Danny Rosenthal was a
friend of my father's who could put a cigarette in his ear
and make smoke come out of his mouth. The only problem that I could see that he had at the moment was that a
singular large adult testicle was trapped like a dead rat
outside the lining of his bathing suit. Danny Rosenthal

was totally oblivious to this matter, but it delighted me as a child, and because of a rather unfortunate state of arrested sexual development, continues to hold the same fascination for me now. Danny Rosenthal's testicle, indeed, hangs suspended like a sun over the happy memories of the last days in the lifetime of my childhood.

You don't see people's testicles hanging out of their bathing suits much anymore. Styles have changed, people have changed, the world's a different kind of place, they say. Instead of looking up at things we now spend most of our time looking down on them. Another reason we don't have Danny Rosenthal's testicle to kick around anymore is that people don't appear to have any balls these days. Balls, like imagination, seem to shrivel with age.

As far as Danny Rosenthal is concerned, I believe I remember my father saying that he stepped on a rainbow some years back. If that is indeed the case I'm sure he's now swimming in the sky with his wayward testicle relegated in the way of all flesh to the shadows on the walls of Hiroshima. I've never told anyone about this small incident of a small child, least of all Danny Rosenthal, but I'm sure he's long past the mortal stage in which social embarrassment might have been incurred. I believe God watches over every testicle, even those that sometimes, quite involuntarily, stray from the herd. I believe that all of us will some day be swimming in the sky with Danny Rosenthal, or at least wind up in a bar somewhere singing Jimmy Buffet cover songs.

To my left and to my right the phones were now ringing. I puffed on the cigar a bit longer, then half dreamily picked up the blower on the left.

"Are you *there?*" said Rambam, with a seemingly urgent intensity in his voice

"Where else would I be?" I said.

CHAPTER TWENTY-NINE

"I THINK I've got something," said Rambam.

"What took you so long?" I said.

I knew Rambam's hard-boiled computer technique could sometimes yield rapid results, but this was ridiculous. I'd given him the list of Willie's exes only the night before as he'd left the loft. Now he was telling me he'd gotten something? It was only half past Gary Cooper time. The espresso machine hadn't even started humming the second verse of "Lara's Theme" from *Dr. Zhivago* yet.

"I won't try to explain to you how the hard-boiled computer method works," said Rambam. "You wouldn't understand the computer part of it and the hard-boiled part of it you wouldn't want to know."

"Correctimundo on both counts," I said, as I watched a stream of blue-gray cigar smoke eddy upward toward the thankfully silent Isle of Lesbos in the heavens one floor above. In New York, I reflected, not only did walls have ears, but ceilings and floors as well often maintained mysterious anthropomorphic Anne Frank–like relationships.

"Now for the time being," Rambam was saying, "let's forget about the girlfriends, lovers, and old flames and let's concentrate on the actual wife and ex-wives. They're the ones with the possible ax to grind, financially, legally, and emotionally, in that special way that only husbands and wives can despise each other."

"Why do you think I live with a cat? What've you got?"

"First of all, he's only been married four times, not ninety-seven times—"

"All right, I exaggerated."

"There were Martha, Shirley, Connie, and the current spouse, Annie. Martha, of course, is dead, though you apparently didn't think that was important enough to mention to me."

"There's no such thing as death," I said.

"Obviously, you've never seen one of your own performances on stage at the Lone Star Cafe."

My mind went back in time about a decade's worth to the last year or two I'd regularly worked the Lone Star. The crowds, the beer-stained floor of the dressing room, the cocaine, the women who'd come and gone, often quite literally, and the few with the hearts of gold who'd hung on like a dying chord until even they knew the dream was over.

"Why do you think I live with a cat?" I said.

"Well," said Rambam, "I know one cat you damned sure won't be wanting to live with."

"The Cat in the Hat?"

"No, Kinky. This cat is an Italian cat. He belongs to a rather interesting family, he knows all about the streets, and, if you reward him properly, he's been known to go out and scratch someone off the book of life for you."

I puffed the cigar thoughtfully and wondered where Rambam was going with this and whether his final destination was going to be a place that would be healthy for young kids and green plants. Rambam had a habit of never telling you everything and at times it could be quite maddening. Like looking for the tie that binds the edge of night to all my children.

"Are you *there?*" said Rambam.

"Yeah. I'm just trying to make an executive decision."

"Which is?"

"Whether to send this cat after Stephanie DuPont or Ratso."

"That's an easy one. When in doubt, always sent a cat after a rat. But I'm afraid this cat's not available. I think he's already got a gig."

"Go on," I said, a bit uneasily.

"Well, it appears as if all the girls Willie's loved before may not feel the same way about him. According to the bank transactions I chased through the hard-boiled computer, which is almost never wrong, wives number two and three each fed this cat very generously just the week before Ben Dorsey was shot."

"Hold the weddin'!" I said.

"Hold the weddin' is right," said Rambam. "If Willie'd just kept on singing through his nose instead of playing with his hose, none of this shit would've happened."

"I'll tell him when I see him. You're sure the computer's got its facts right? I mean, a conspiracy of ex-wives is almost as hard to believe as Lee Harvey Oswald acting alone from the top of the Texas Cookbook Suppository. How much did the exes supposedly pay this—uh—cat?"

"There's no supposedly. They paid him ten thousand dollars apiece."

"Mother of God," I ejaculated. "That's all it costs to whack somebody these days?"

"You can get a decent hit for that. Or scare the living shit out of somebody. Life's cheap, Kinky."

"Life may be cheap, my lad, but it can be rich in the coin of the spirit."

"Try buying cat food and cigars with the coin of the spirit. In a couple of weeks time you and the cat'd be living out of that Dumpster on Vandam Street."

"That's all right. We'd pretend we were on a ship with Dr. Dolittle searching for the giant pink sea snail."

"Then the men in the little white suits would come—"

"That's all right. The cat would keep me company in wig city just like Van Gogh had a cat in the mental hospital to keep him company—"

"He also had an ear to keep him company—"

"Everyone in wig city should have a cat," I continued tirelessly, "to keep him company, and everybody else should have a cat so that when they start talking to themselves all the time they won't realize they're crazy."

"Which is what this whole situation with the ex-wives putting out a hit on Willie is, I'll admit. But I'm going to look into it further for two reasons. One: the hard-boiled computer is never, in a technical sense, wrong. And two: when you've got a client whose entire life's credo is 'Fuck 'em if they can't take a joke,' anything's possible. Now how are you coming along on the Indians?"

"Just saddling up. But back to this Italian cat for a moment. The only Italians I know are Dylan Ferrero, Christopher Columbus, and Pope Witch-burner the Elder, who ascended to the papacy following Pope Turbo-dick the Second—"

"Those aren't the only Italians you know. You know another one indirectly. The one who gave you your espresso machine."

After cradling the blower I sat at my desk for a while, smoking the cigar and contemplating the rather ornate commercial espresso machine that took up about a third of my kitchen. It had finished with Dr. Zhivago and was now busily humming away on a theme very much akin to "The March of the Siamese Children" from *The King and I*, a sure sign that it was approaching about as close to a sexual climax as an espresso machine ever gets.

I remembered the day, some years ago, when the men had come to install the huge, shiny dingus. Later I'd learned it'd been sent to me as a gift from a man whose daughter I'd rescued from a mugging at an automated bank on Christopher Street. Rambam had told me it was not necessary, or even particularly advisable, to call the man or send him a thank-you note. He was, according to Rambam, the kind of guy you appreciate from a distance.

His name was Joe the Hyena.

I couldn't believe that Shirley and Connie, the latter of whom I'd met on several occasions, could possibly be in collusion to whack Willie. It was the craziest thing I'd ever heard, yet what other connection, especially coming just prior to the Ben Dorsey affair, could they have possibly had with a man like Joe the Hyena? Even Rambam stayed the hell away from Joe the Hyena.

"Koo-koo-kah-choo," said the espresso machine, possibly in defense of Joe the Hyena.

"Koo-koo-kah-choo," I explained to the cat, "is a phrase that either Paul Simon lifted from the Beatles song 'The Walrus,' or the Beatles borrowed from the Paul Simon song 'Mrs. Robinson.' Nobody knows or cares which anymore except myself and John Lennon."

It was fairly obvious that the cat did not care which. It was also fairly obvious that the espresso machine itself was only seconds away from building up enough internal combustion to blast off the counter like a booster rocket, launch itself through the cigar-smoke-laden ionosphere of the loft, crash through the ceiling, and lodge its burning cauldron of love directly into the middle of Winnie Katz's lesbian dance class like a giant gleaming phallus.

"What a waste," I said to the cat.

The cat fixed me with a cold, psychic, feminine eye. As always, she was quick to misconstrue my meaning.

"I meant," I said pointedly, "all that espresso."

CHAPTER THIRTY

I SPENT the rest of the afternoon chasing Indians around in the dust of the loft, listening to lesbians on the roof, drinking cup after cup of hot, bitter espresso, and puffing on enough Cuban cigars to feed a family almost as big as Willie's. The cat had sat on the desk for a while, giving me the old fish-eye as the cigar smoke curled up toward the ceiling. When she'd had enough of that, she jumped off the desk and onto the kitchen table, where she continued to aim a gaze of rather intense malice toward the back of my head. I couldn't actually see it, but I could feel the heat.

Cats do not like cigar smoke as a rule and they are especially put out about Cuban cigar smoke. The reason for this is really very simple. Cats know that, along with Jews and newspaper publishers, they are in the top three categories of people that dictators and despots despise. There is something in the cat's freewheeling, independent nature that invariably gets up the sleeve of all power-driven pricks. Hitler liked dogs but he hated cats. Napoleon hated cats. Alexander the Great hated cats. Idi Amin hated cats. On the other hand, the Prophet Mohammed loved cats so much that he cut the sleeve off his robe with a sharp dagger rather than waken his cat and still made it to the mosque on time. Albert Schweitzer, who already had a rather hideous handwriting, wrote prescriptions with whichever arm his cat was not reclining upon. Winston

Churchill reportedly refused to eat, drink, sleep, or take a Nixon (of course, it wasn't called a Nixon back then) unless his cat, Jock, could be present for the event. On one particularly unpleasant occasion, when Jock ran away for a fortnight, Churchill became quite constipated, emotionally distraught, and rude to Lady Astor until Jock returned just in time for D-Day or "Dump Day" as Churchill called it, when he laid some serious transatlantic cable. And the ubiquitous Van Gogh remained a free spirit even when local frogs began wondering "Where did Vincent Van Gogh?" He didn't go anywhere, but history does record that he came quite a bit. He was masturbating like a monkey in the mental hospital, but he still had his cat, who reportedly wore a little green accountant's visor so as not to witness these incessant acts of human depravity.

Given all this, it's not really surprising that any cat with a brain the size of a small Welsh mining town would not like Fidel Castro and would find Cuban cigar smoke a rather repellent symbol of totalitarianism. The cat's eyes now seemed to be reflecting a peculiarly green anarchistic glow.

"Politics has nothing to do with it," I said to the cat. "I just like to smoke Cuban cigars."

The cat, in a final gesture of disgust, turned her back on me and sat very erect upon the kitchen table staring intently in the direction of the puppet head. For its part, the puppet head seemed to smile back in secret understanding.

"I'm not supporting their economy," I said. "I'm burning their fields."

The cat, of course, said nothing.

The afternoon, however, was not all Cuban cigar smoke and bathroom mirrors. When the puppet head was not smiling its smarmy, sympathetic smile, and the cat wasn't busy doggedly endeavoring to distract me, I was

able somehow to effectuate a good bit of work on the
blower. I'd spoken to Doug Holloway, gotten a bit more
background on the bus accident, and asked him to keep
digging. I'd left a message for Willie on the bus, which
was now parked across the street from Bobbie's house
near the golf course at Briarcliff. Willie was home for a
few days of much needed rest and, according to Doug,
was now playing about seven hundred rounds of golf. This
was good, because I did not look forward to discussing the
Joe the Hyena situation with him just at the moment. It
had to be done, however. It's always a good idea to alert
your client to his possible imminent destruction at the
hands of former wives. It makes good business sense, too.

I also left a message at the Connecticut office of
Willie's manager, Mark Rothbaum. I'd heard on the honeysuckle vine that Mark had some rather outlandish theory
about Willie's involvement with the Indians and I was
ready to hear it. I liked to hear outlandish theories and I
wanted to see if this one could top Rambam's. I might
have to wait a while, however. Mark Rothbaum was a
manager and he'd known since he was a small child the
wisdom of never returning calls too promptly. Could be a
cold day in Jerusalem before I heard from him. I wasn't
sure I had that long.

The other possibly significant call I'd made that afternoon was to my Native American friend Robby Romero,
who lived in a cabin outside Taos, New Mexico. Robby
had been born and raised by the Apache Indians with a
little help from Dennis Hopper, Dean Stockwell, and, I
liked to think, myself. He had one foot in the white man's
world, but his heart had definitely been buried at
Wounded Knee. If anybody could help me cipher the
meaning of the contents of the parcel wrapped in buckskin, it was Robby.

Unfortunately, Robby was not on the res, as the

young girl told me when I called and asked of his whereabouts. When I told her it was important she said, "He's
heading to where the sun comes up." When I emphasized
the urgency of the matter again, she said, "All right, I'll
call him on his pager." I gave her my address and phone
number and she assured me Robby would be in touch as
soon as possible.

After a long day's work on the blower with damned
little to show for it, I was beginning to have my doubts
about the wisdom of taking on the investigation in the first
place. I put on my blue Oliver Twist overcoat and cowboy
hat, grabbed three cigars for the road, and left the cat in
charge. It was a cold night in a cold world, I thought, as I
walked the misty, muffled streets in the definite direction
of nowhere. I was all alone in this thing and if I made the
wrong move I'd be powerless to prevent the enemy from
attacking the king.

I wandered vaguely toward Little Italy, smoking a
cigar, meeting no one, keeping my hands warm in the
pockets of my overcoat, and my mind, cold and rational
and open to the wind. I didn't have the FBI, the local
police, or even some promoter's concert security force to
back me up. Clearly, someone would very likely try again.
If there was any pattern, motive, or rationale in this I had
to find it pretty fast. And one luxury I didn't have was
guessing wrong.

I didn't much like the ex-wives theory that the hard-
boiled computer had spit out and Rambam was now, hopefully, running down. The idea of an Indian curse seemed
even more outlandish. And there were a myriad of dark
spaces in Willie's chess-and-checkered career that I had
neither the time nor the resources to explore. Maybe a
jealous boyfriend or husband was involved. Maybe another
long-ago songwriter who was down on his luck and felt
Willie had stolen his material. That happened a lot in

Nashville back in the symbiotic old song-swapping days. Maybe a disgruntled postal worker had gotten his zip codes mixed up. Maybe some fan had just overidentified with his field of study. Maybe some guy had a few too many birds on his television antenna. Maybe the whole situation was like Willie's song. Crazy.

It's not supposed to be this way, I thought. The shotgun Willie approach could take you off in a million directions at once, only to leave you nowhere at all and drowning in yesterday's wine. Rambam had been right. If all you've got is ex-wives and Indians, those are the ghost herds you've got to ride after. Rambam had a good Jewish nose for the criminal spoor. I'd successfully followed Rambam's nose before and I figured I might as well follow it again. I just hoped it would lead to somewhere soon. If not, this investigation could turn out to be a real booger.

I was fresh out of charm by the time I got to Luna's on Mulberry Street. I told the guy at the door: "Sirhan Sirhan, party of one." He didn't bat an eye, just led me to a table of roughly the size, shape, and stability of a chess board on a bus. I looked around and didn't feel too bad, however. There were lots of parties of one it seemed, some of whom, no doubt, were just people like myself, busy chasing Indians of their own invention.

What seemed like many moons and meatballs later, powered largely by natural gas, I was able to make my way back to Vandam Street. It was closing in on Cinderella time and a strong sense of normal New York paranoia appeared to be pervading my mind. Shadows without people attached seemed to be skulking and scurrying between all the buildings and behind every lamppost. By the time I got to the loft I felt like Ichabod Crane on opening night.

"I'm jumpy as a cat," I said to the cat, as I opened

the kitchen window wide enough to let out the residual cigar smoke and evil spirits.

The cat, of course, said nothing.

Then, as I walked over to the counter to shake hands with the Jameson bottle, something highly irregular, even for New York, occurred. From somewhere in the darkness a shaft of wood fairly zimmed through the open window and lodged, still quivering, in the ceiling. It was a brightly feathered arrow, and while its sudden intrusion proved mildly unnerving to me, the cat seemed to be positively enjoying its presence in the loft.

"Just as I suspected," I said. "All dogs are cowboys and all cats are Indians."

Then a very authentic-sounding Indian war cry reverberated throughout Vandam Street, quite possibly, for the first time in several hundred years.

CHAPTER THIRTY-ONE

A SHORT WHILE later, with the arrow still embedded in the ceiling and the lesbian dance class going at it in such a way as to make the bright feathers tremble ever so slightly, two proud young Native Americans were seated at the kitchen table of my humble old loft. Robby Romero and his friend Benito had been travelling with Robby's band, Red Thunder and, as the Wind God or whoever was in charge of these things would have it, they'd been in New York City meeting with illustrious MTV representatives at just about the time I'd tried to reach Robby in New Mexico. Having gotten my phone number and address from the girl on the res, it'd been quite easy for them to lie in wait somewhere along Vandam Street and then scare the shit out of a middle-aged Jewish white man by firing an arrow through the open window. All this notwithstanding, and ever the courteous host, I offered them both a place to stay for the night, a couple of good cigars, and their choice of espresso or firewater.

"Thanks," said Robby, "but MTV's putting us up while we're in the city."

"Where?"

"The Plaza."

"Great," I said. "Maybe the cat and I can crash with you."

"You're both welcome," said Benito.

"But we'll pass on the firewater," said Robby. "Every Indian is not a drunk, Kinky."

"You can stitch that one on a blanket," I said. "Now how about some espresso and cigars?"

Both young men nodded, so I walked over and kicked the espresso machine into gear. Within moments it was busily humming its own inimitable version of "Running Bear," which did not seem especially politically correct, but who's going to stand there and argue with an espresso machine. I went back over to the desk, took two good Cuban cigars out of Sherlock's porcelain head, and gave them to my surprise guests.

"Offering tobacco's very thoughtful," said Robby. "It means you're learning our traditional ways."

"That's right," I said. "Nothing like a little Indian ambush in the middle of the night to make you a fast learner."

"That *was* a hell of a shot, Benito," said Robby admiringly.

"Especially," said Benito, "since I had to fire over the garbage trucks."

"By the way, fellas," I said as I brought the espresso, "what'd you do with the bow? Leave it in the limo?"

Robby and Benito laughed. Benito stood up and reached for a leather saddlebag. He removed a small tubular object.

"It's a take-apart bow," he said, quickly assembling the dingus, to the great interest of the cat and the moderate interest of myself.

"Anybody tries to mug you," I said, "he may find himself walking around with an arrow through his scrotum."

"If he's lucky," said Benito. "Actually, these are nothing new. The Turks had them in the eleventh century."

"Ah, the wonderfully inventive Turks," I said, lighting a fresh cigar and putting a new head on everybody's espresso. "They massacred one and a half million Armenians, machine-gunned thousands of ammo-less Aussies at Gallipoli, and as if that wasn't enough, they bull-fucked Lawrence of Arabia. That's a pretty impressive record."

"Almost as impessive as the white man's," said Robby, puffing coolly on his cigar.

The easy bantering at this point degenerated into an intense argument between myself and Robby, as always insoluble, as always generating a good bit more heat than light. Benito, who'd seen this behavioral cycle occur only once before at the Del Norte Restaurant in Kerrville, Texas, looked on with slightly bemused enjoyment like a lawn tennis spectator watching a rally that keeps increasing in intensity while at the same time seems as if it's never going to end. The crux of the argument was always the same. Robby contended that the white man was the source of all the woes in the world and I contended that the white man was similar to Babe Ruth: if you hit more home runs than anyone else you're also going to strike out more than anyone else.

"At least," said Robby, "you're not calling me at seven o'clock in the morning like you did when we lived in Hollywood and saying: 'Wake up! I've got a rock of cocaine as big as your dick.'"

"Unfortunately," I said, "you never woke up."

"Probably saved my life."

"The Cocaine God was unable, even through the wiles of the white man, to tempt you. And now the Private Investigation God has brought you to my door. I need your help, Robby."

It was true. If Robby Romero couldn't help me shed some light into the black hole of this investigation, I didn't know who could. A trusted friend of mine, and wise to the ways of the white man, Robby had a unique and privileged inside track with the tribal elders as well. He was not bitter. He was not a sellout. He was still a warrior fighting the good fight for his people as he saw it. And, maybe most important of all, he'd walked his own private trail of tears. Now, if I could just get him to walk one more mile for the Kinkster.

I gave Robby and Benito a quick *Reader's Digest* version of the Willie situation. The bus accident in Arizona that killed the Indian. The mysterious Indian messenger delivering the buckskin package in Florida. The bullet in Buffalo that had hit Ben Dorsey but almost surely had had Willie's name on it. The Indian Ben claimed to have seen outside the hotel room window before he'd gotten shot.

"So you think someone's trying to get back at Willie for the guy who was killed in Arizona?" said Robby.

"Well, I think you'll agree there is sort of a Native American motif here. Possibly, it's a bit far-fetched—"

"It's very far-fetched," said Robby. "In fact, I think it's fucked. Native Americans support Willie and Willie supports Native Americans. He's widely known as a friend to the Indian. He's helped us lots of times, done benefits, helped protect the Black Hills and the sacred lands, done a concert for Leonard Peltier who the feds accused of being a cop-killer but was really just defending his home. As I recall, Willie took a lot of shit from the feds and the law enforcement community as a result."

"Look, Robby, just because Willie's sympathies obviously lie with the Indians doesn't mean that *every* Indian feels the same about him. Just as I can't speak for every Jew—thank Christ—you can't speak for every Indian."

"But I know someone who can," said Robby.

"Can what?"

"Speak for every Indian."

"Take me to your leader," I said.

"We may have to dig him up and use him as a hand puppet," said Robby.

"Then we could give him to the Smithsonian," I said.

CHAPTER THIRTY-TWO

As you might've suspected, Robby did not take me to his leader. For one thing, it was two-thirty in the morning and any leader worth following was no doubt seriously on the nod by this time. For another, I'd fallen off the espresso wagon at sometime earlier in the evening and segued neatly over to the firewater and that was how I'd been drinking it. Neatly. It didn't take the Chief Proctologist of the Semihole Nation to determine that I'd travelled a bridge too far and now was on the verge, or should we say rim, of becoming a latent asshole.

The cat, always alert for the very slightest behavioral changes, seemed to be somewhat put off. But Robby, for his part, did not seem to mind or even take much notice. Long ago he and I had come to the conclusion that the only people in life that were truly worth knowing were the assholes. They're usually smarter and more consistent, and you never waste any time wondering if they're just trying to be nice.

Robby was now smoking a fresh cigar and rocking back and forth in the rocking chair like a man in deep meditation. I'd relit an ancient half-smoked cigar that had fallen behind my desk and now I was in full pacing mode up and down the living-room floor. The cat was now sitting on the kitchen table watching both of us rather suspiciously. And, for his part, Benito had taken a break from both of our harangues and was nodding out for a while on the couch. It wasn't the Plaza, but it'd have to do.

"You're asking me who might do this," said Robby. "Throughout history there've always been sellouts. Every culture has them. In our case they've taken the form of traitors, turncoats, Indian scouts, all of whom sell their own people down the river—sometimes literally—to aid and abet the white man, always for a price. The only good thing about it was that often the double-crossers got double-crossed themselves. So it could well be someone like this. Some individual or rogue group that is not acting under the orders or with the knowledge of the tribal authorities."

"Then it might be a bitch to find whoever's behind this."

"Not necessarily. We pretty well know who these people are. If we don't, we have ways to find out."

"Then you have ways to make them talk."

"Damn straight," said Robby. "But that's not what's worrying me."

I puffed the cigar and continued pacing back and forth across the dusty wooden floor. Robby continued rocking silently back and forth in the rocking chair. Benito continued to snore lightly on the couch. The cat continued to watch me pacing back and forth, occasionally casting a rather jaundiced eye toward Robby, who'd unknowingly appropriated her rocking chair. The lesbian dance class continued to hammer away on the floor or the ceiling above, whichever story you wanted to believe.

"What the hell's going on upstairs?" asked Robby.

"Lesbian dance class."

"How do you know they're lesbians?"

"How do you know they're not?"

"Same way I know every Indian is not a drunk."

"I'll drink to that," I said, as I walked over to what

was left of the bottle of Jameson and poured a healthy shot into the bull's horn. I killed the shot and looked out over old Vandam Street with fire in my eyes. "So what's worrying you, Robby?" I said.

"Well, maybe there's someone else out there."

"There's lots of someone elses out there."

"Yeah, but I mean maybe there's someone who doesn't like to see America's number one cowboy riding with the Indians."

"That's a pipe dream, Robby. There's nothing here to suggest it. The bus hits an Indian. An Indian messenger brings Willie the package. Ben resembles Willie from a distance. Ben goes into Willie's suite at the hotel. Ben sees an Indian. Ben gets shot. If we don't get to the bottom of this pretty soon there may not be anyone around to ride off into the sunset."

Robby remained silent, just rocking back and forth and staring straight ahead like a man in a peyote dream. I walked over to the desk and opened a drawer and removed the parcel that the Indian had given to Willie and Willie had given to me. I began unwrapping the thing as I brought it back to Robby.

"Then, of course, we have this item on loan from the Willie Nelson Nightmare Collection," I said. "Check out this little booger, will you?"

I started to place it in Robby's lap then I suddenly noticed he wasn't in the chair anymore. A true instance had occurred, apparently, of a man leaping sideways.

"*Put that thing away!*" he shouted. "*Where the hell did you get that?*"

"I told you the Indian came up to the bus and gave this to Willie in Florida. Then Willie—"

"*Don't touch it!*"

"How do you expect me to put this bastard away if I don't touch it?"

At this point Benito and the cat became involved in the situation, the cat jumping off the kitchen table and reclaiming the rocking chair and Benito suddenly sitting up on the couch like a zombie arising.

"What're you doing with that smoked hide?" he shouted. "Where the hell did you get that?"

"I was trying to tell Robby. The Indian gave it to Willie and Willie—"

"This is the worst thing you could have taken possession of," said Benito, moving away from the rocking chair as if it were radioactive. "It's very bad medicine. It's other man's medicine."

"It's other nation's medicine," added Robby. "It's not even from the Southwest."

"Well, what the hell does it mean?" I said. Not only was I fresh out of horsepitality at the moment, I was also beginning to feel little insects creeping along my spine.

"It means we're getting out of here," said Robby. "This is too spooky."

"Hold the weddin'!" I shouted. "You guys can't just walk out of here and leave me alone with this thing."

In truth, they could, and that's what they appeared to be doing. But the whole scenario seemed so incredible. Here were two intelligent, strong, young men who suddenly seemed transformed into the mind-set of small, frightened boys. And for some reason I couldn't quite cipher, I wasn't looking forward too eagerly to spending the night alone in the loft myself. Only the cat appeared to have the situation under control, lying calmly in the rocking chair, watching guardedly as our guests headed for the door.

"Don't leave," I shouted, as if to a lover.

Robby and Benito did not answer. They were conferring nervously in the open doorway. This gave me a moment to rewrap the object I still held in my hands and think things over just a bit. The people that had seen the contents of the package thus far had all been white men. Myself, Rambam, Willie, and possibly Ben and Just Bill. Robby and Benito had been the first Native Americans to shovel a glimpse and what they'd seen had evidently been enough to frighten the daylights out of them. It was other man's medicine, all right, but that didn't mean I had to take it lying down. In fact, I wasn't sure how I was going to sleep tonight. The place had suddenly gotten very quiet. Even the lesbian dance class had ceased its incessant activities. Only the traffic and the nighttime street noise of the city still seemed to steadily permeate the walls of the loft like the dreadful drone of the drums of war.

Before I knew what was happening Robby had come back over to me carrying what looked like some kind of ceremonial blanket. His hands were shaking slightly.

"Give it to me," he said. "We're going to smudge the whole fucking place."

Behind him Benito had set fire to a stick he was carrying and a strange, sweet smell started to override the cigar-smoke-laden loft. It did not smell like New York.

"This is a smudge stick," said Benito, as if explaining to a child or a white man. "We're burning cedar, sage, and sweetgrass. Just relax and stay where you are. We're going to smudge you, too."

"Smudge away," I said.

Using the smudge stick and a brightly beaded eagle feather fan Benito began wafting the sweet-smelling smoke gently over everyone and everything in sight. Like the wing that it was, the eagle fan touched my shoulders ever so slightly. Even for a white man, I could feel its power. Like spiritual soap. Benito was now muttering softly and sweetly to himself with Robby joining in occasionally and the loft filling up with the pure, all-pervasive presence of the burning sage. For me the feeling was very similar to that of a two-man minyan chanting the Kaddish.

"Watch," said Robby, as Benito neared the rocking chair, smudging things you could see and, no doubt, those that you couldn't. "The cat will dig the vibe."

This was putting it a bit mildly, for the cat reverted to excited, innocent kittenhood the moment Benito began to smudge her. She ran around the room and rolled on the floor in a playful frenzy I hadn't seen since Christ was a Comanche.

"She thinks it's catnip," said Benito.

"Maybe it is," said Robby.

Sometime later, Benito had wrapped the medicine bundle containing the smudge stick and eagle feather fan in cloths of various bright colors and put it away. Robby had deep-sixed the smoked-hide package in his saddlebag and agreed to take it to "Tadodaho," chief of the six-nation Iroquois Confederacy at Onondaga, near Syracuse, New York. It was right on their way, he explained. Red Thunder's Call to Action Tour to protect the sacred lands was scheduled to play Syracuse next anyway.

"At least the Travel Agent God is with us," I said.

"No shit," said Robby. "But it still doesn't make sense. This thing looks Iroquois to me and the guy killed in Arizona almost certainly was Hopi or Navajo. I'll find that out for you, but either way I don't understand why the medicine's Iroquois."

"The smudging service is on the house," said Benito.

"In more ways than one," I said, as I embraced Robby and shook hands with Benito at the door.

"Just one more thing," said Robby. "If this shit turns out to be authentic you'll have to call off your investigation."

"I can't do that, Robby."

"You'll have to, sooner or later."

"Why?"

"Because if the medicine's real the person it was intended for will die very slowly and very painfully and there will be absolutely nothing any of us can do about it."

CHAPTER THIRTY-THREE

MAYBE WE'LL ALL have our fifteen minutes of fame. But time, of course, is the money of fame. And time, as Albert Einstein observed when he wasn't busy looking for his bicycle in Princeton, New Jersey, is relative. Therefore, my fellow members of the slide-rule club, my fellow passengers on this ship of fools, we are forced to draw the following conclusion: We may all have our fifteen minutes of fame, but Edith Piaf's fifteen minutes is likely to run on a little longer than Vanilla Ice's fifteen minutes. Nevertheless, when everybody's time and fame has all run out and Lovely Rita Meter Maid, Former Miss Texas 1987, finally waltzes up and embraces us at the end of the troubled dream, we will all die alone in hopeless, courageous oblivion like Gauguin or Tiny Tim. And when the end comes at last, each and every one of us will have at least one comforting thought as we fall through that timeless trapdoor: Albert Einstein is still probably out there somewhere looking for his fucking bicycle.

These were my reflections the following morning as I struggled to light my first cigar of the day with the sweet, pungent smell of sage hanging over my latest hangover. Fame could be fleeting, I figured, especially for those who've spent a lifetime pursuing it only to see it evaporate faster than the foggy, foggy dew, like the dream that it truly is, like so much cigar smoke in a dusty loft. Yet for those few who find lasting fame within their lifetime, things can sometimes be even more frustrating. If you think it's hard living with who you are, try living with who you've become.

The fact that Willie Nelson was one of the most famous people in the world did not make it any easier to conduct an investigation for him or of him. In many ways it made things more difficult. For one thing, everybody, including myself, felt as if they knew him far better than they actually did. Willie's life was like a Bible story you grew up with. You'd known all about it since you were a child. Nothing would ever change your own personal version of the story. Nothing could ever go wrong, and if it ever did, everything would work out fine in the end. Of course, a lot of people died in the Bible and a hell of a lot more died because of it.

The other problem was that Willie's fame shone with such brilliance that it often kept those around him from seeing the light. I was having some problems in that department myself at the moment. This investigation, if you wanted to call it that, was powering ahead on twin tracks with each train of thought seemingly more ridiculous than the other. At this rate both of them should be plunging off the bridge of my nose into Lake Stupid at just about the same time. The evidence seemed so flimsy and the two theories so preposterous that it would almost feel like a social embarrassment right now to have to discuss the case with my client. On the other hand, was it right to keep wild Indians and vengeful ex-wives running around in your head when your client's life might be in danger?

I was just nursing my first cup of espresso out of the machine when the phones rang. Possibly it was Rambam with some more data to back up or cast asparagus upon his fairly incredible findings. Possibly, Doug Holloway or Just Bill, who I understood was also looking into things, had some further information on the accident in Arizona.

Possibly the manager, Mark Rothbaum, was calling to bare his businesslike bosom to me regarding his vaunted theories about red men and redheaded strangers. Possibly, my pal Robby Romero had taken the red-eye to Syracuse and was calling to report that he had the case all wrapped up by now.

In fact, there was only one person I dreaded speaking to just now. That was my client, America's number one cowboy who was busy racking up ex-wives and riding with the Indians and, very probably by this time, looking for a few answers. With the cigar in my mouth and the espresso in my left hand, I picked up the blower on the right. It's always a bit of a spiritual blunder to pick up the blower on the right and this time was no exception.

"Start talkin'," I said.

"Large Dick," said the familiar, fabled, mellifluous tones. "What have you got?"

PART FOUR

MAN

"There are only two stories in all of
literature—a man goes on a journey,
a stranger comes to town."

—TOLSTOY

CHAPTER THIRTY-FOUR

WHAT'VE I GOT?" I said. "I've got an unpleasant hangover, a cold loft, a hungry cat, and a rather troubling bout of projectile diarrhea."

"Sorry to hear that," said Willie. "But have you found anything out yet?"

"Yeah," I said. "I've found out that I've got to take a growler in a few minutes. Everything including my bowels seems to be moving along pretty damn quickly."

"That's great," said Willie. "But do you have any hot leads?"

"Hot leads? Jesus Christ, Uncle Willie, I've only been on the job a couple of days. Some rather interesting patterns are beginning to suggest themselves, but I wouldn't say I had any hot leads just yet."

"That's good to hear," said Willie. "So you'll keep diggin' up bones?"

"Till she gets the gold mine and I get the shaft," I said.

I might've been wrong but I thought I was detecting a measure of relief in Willie's voice. Relief that I hadn't stumbled on any hot leads yet. When he changed the subject abruptly, I was sure of it.

"I've been down here relaxing, just playing some golf, you know. So I was hanging out in the pro shop this morning and a woman came in complaining she was stung by a bee. So the golf pro asked her where she'd gotten stung.

She told him it was between the first and the second holes. So he says: 'I can tell you right now your stance is too wide.' "

It was fairly early in the morning and I hadn't laughed in about a hundred and eleven years so I hadn't really planned on convulsing to death with mirth at the end of this particular anecdote. It wasn't really all that funny when you stopped to think about it. But when you stop to think about things, very few of them are terribly funny. It was, in fact, just humorous enough to make me burn my upper lip on my cup of espresso and to cry out—the clinical term for which is "to bark" in the frighteningly peculiar manner of the Tourette's Syndrome victim. Willie, unfortunately, thought I was shouting the word "What?"

"I can tell you right now your stance is too wide," he said.

I chuckled along good-naturedly and tried to think of a few questions a private investigator who didn't have any hot leads might ask a client who might not be too eager for the case to be solved. There was no point in alarming the client by conjuring up a conspiracy of wicked wives and wild Indians projectile-vomiting bile and bad medicine as they fucked, sucked, cajoled, and galloped their way round and round in a terrible, ever-tightening carousel of death. On the other hand, a private investigator was hardly worthy of the name if he couldn't confront his cosmic client with a cryptic question or two.

"Willie," I said, pausing to sip some espresso and puff my cigar, "there's just a couple things I'd like to clear up if I could."

"Smudge away," he said.

A cold current seemed to flow through the loft, simultaneously filling my veins with ice and my senses with sage. Even a cosmic client like Willie had no right to be telepathic. But maybe Sammy Allred had been right. The guy *was* psychic. I smoked my cigar in stunned wonder for a moment and said nothing.

"It's an Indian thing," said Willie.

It certainly was, I thought. It had also been my precise words to Benito the night before. For a desolate few seconds I considered the notion that Willie the wanderin' gypsy had been watching from the bathroom mirror, but I quickly rejected it. It had to be coincidence. In the pale light of the twentieth century we call a lot of things coincidence. Yet there seemed to be some hidden lyrics here. Some songs Willie wasn't singing to me. If I wanted to win the Wurlitzer prize I was going to have to walk across the dusty barroom floor of his life and pump a few coins of the spirit into that incandescent jukebox of his memory. The old chess game between us was continuing, it seemed. Neither of us telling the other, apparently, what was always on his mind.

"Look, Willie," I said, "let's forget the Indians for a moment—"

"Everybody else has," he said.

"I'd just like to know if all your exes still live in Texas."

I knew, of course, that they didn't. Shirley now lived in Branson, Missouri, the dinosaur graveyard of country music, which was probably still better than what you hear on the radio, and Connie currently lived in San Diego, where I left a stepladder once and a piece of my heart. I just wanted to get Willie's take on Connie and Shirley without telling him they might be plotting to cap him. They might, for all I knew, be plotting to kill Caesar. The whole sordid matter had to be a mistake, but it still needed looking into.

"As a matter of fact they don't," Willie said, "and I like to keep it that way. They can't poison the water for future wives. That's the one good thing about getting married. Every time I do it, all my old lines are good again."

"Do Connie and Shirley know each other?"

"Ask them."

"Don't worry."

Willie seemed deliberately obstructive now. I'd talk to Connie and Shirley all right. I kind of felt sorry for them anyway. Always having to listen to Willie's music in elevators and dentists' waiting rooms. It couldn't be easy.

"By the way, Willie, until we speak again, just a word to the wise: Beware of Indians and ex-wives."

"Always good advice."

"We should have some kind of break in this investigation soon and when we do you'll be the first to know. It's also possible that the whole thing may just dry up and blow away and amount to nothing to worry about."

"In that case," said Willie, "I'll just spend the rest of my life working on my Ben Crenshaw impersonation."

"Like they say, the good thing about golf is it's the only chance Republicans have to dress up like pimps and get away with it."

"I don't know about Republicans," said Willie, "but I do want to be a pimp when I grow up."

"Your foreskin is ready, Mr. Nelson," said a voice in the background that I recognized as belonging to Doug Holloway.

"Got to run, Big Dick," said Willie. "Gotta beat that little white pellet around for a couple of hours. Hey, did I tell you I'm playing New York in a few weeks? We can talk about the case then—if it's still a case. We're doing two nights at Radio City. It's a Farm Aid gig. Farmers are friendly, aren't they?"

"Except for the one in *Charlotte's Web*."

"Probably won't be too many farmers around anyway. New York City's kind of a strange place for a Farm Aid Concert, I guess."

"Not really. There *are* a few things we grow in New York."

"Name one," said Willie.

"Cynical," I said.

CHAPTER THIRTY-FIVE

Is THIS really necessary?" I said to Rambam.

"Of course it's necessary," said Rambam, "if you ever want to be a successful little private investigator. You've got to follow up every lead—even if it leads you nowhere. You can't just go to Connie and Shirley and ask them why they're writing large checks to a man like Joe the Hyena. Sometimes you've got to look the hyena right in the mouth."

"What we're looking at doesn't appear to be his mouth," I said.

It was early in the evening and Rambam and I were having cappuccino and cannoli at a little pastry shop on Mulberry Street, deep in the bullet-riddled Romeo-and-Juliet heart of Little Italy. Our gaze, however, was fixed directly across the street to a depressing, not to say forbidding-looking, little place called the Napoli i Roma Social Club. It was not the kind of club Groucho Marx or almost anyone else would want to be a member of.

"Well," said Rambam, turning his attention briefly back to me, "at least you're looking better than you did before you left on your road trip with Willie. You're almost back to your engaging, positive, gracious self again."

"I'm busy this weekend, if that's what you're thinking."

"*Almost* back," said Rambam. "But seriously, I don't think I've ever seen you looking this well."

I continued to sip my espresso and wrap my choppers around the cannoli and sort of let Rambam's rare effort at praise mingle with the small talk of other conversations and drift away like the rest of the tinny music into the starless sky above Little Italy. It's never a good sign when someone says, "He's never looked better," or "I've never seen him so happy," or similar words to this effect. What usually happens is about three days later they find the well-looking, happy person hanging from a shower rod and then the same person invariably gets to say the same thing all over again only this time in the past tense: "I'd never seen him looking better. He seemed happier than I'd ever seen him in his life." What this demonstrates, most probably, is how little insight most of us have into the condition the human condition is in. Of course, it's not the kind of thing you'd really want to know in the first place. Could just set you off your nice cannoli.

"What makes you so sure that's the place?" I asked, steering the conversation back across to the Napoli i Roma Social Club.

"I don't have time to give you a lecture right now on *The Decline and Fall of the Roman Empire*," said Rambam. "Let's just say that Joe the Hyena's been known to operate out of this place. Also I've pulled the phone records for Connie and Shirley and both of them have made calls to this number several times over the past few months. When I tried to pull the phone records for the Napoli i Roma Social Club the guy at Nynex phone security laughed. 'God!' he said. 'Another copy?' So somebody besides us has been pretty actively looking into the operation."

"The feds?"

"No," said Rambam sarcastically. "It was Little Jimmy Dickens."

"I didn't know you knew that much about country

music," I said, lighting a cigar and looking at Rambam with renewed admiration.

"I know about as much about country music as you know about the Mob," he said.

I puffed on the cigar and shoveled another glimpse across the street. The front of the social club had been painted or tinted up to about eye level so that you couldn't really see in the place but anyone inside could look across the street and see a guy with a big black cowboy hat smoking a cigar. The waiter came by and Rambam and I both moved up the ladder a bit to espressos. Rambam said nothing for a while until the waiter had brought the espressos and he'd taken an initial sip.

"Yours are better," he said, holding the little cup thoughtfully.

"We try to keep the customer satisfied."

"Speaking of customers," said Rambam, "there's a few other little indicators I didn't tell you about."

"Such as?"

"Two canceled checks. One from Connie and one from Shirley."

"Made out to Joe the Hyena?"

"Of course not. That would be too easy. They're made out to the Little Italy Carting and Window Cleaning Company."

"You're kidding."

"I wish I was. Those are two of the biggest rackets the mob has. Everybody knows about the control they exert over the garbage pickup situation. You hire them to pick up the garbage or you get twice as much garbage back. As far as window cleaning goes, you hire them to clean your windows or you find that you don't have windows."

"At least they do windows," I said.

"That's not *all* they do. And it sure as hell ain't what Connie and Shirley hired them for."

We finished our espressos and did what most people do at sidewalk cafes the world over when they're not busy solving the problems of the world. We watched the eager tourists and the cheerful young couples walk obliviously by, as well as one rather persistent young man who appeared to be wandering around in a homosexual fugue. Did they know that storybook monsters like Joe the Hyena might be lurking nearby? Probably. Did they care? Probably not. They wouldn't care if you were Oscar Wilde oozing from every orifice, drunk and disintegrating in historical slow motion outside some Left Bank café in the death-driven rain, too broke to pay the bill, too broken to care about the people passing by. All people passing by know is that milk comes from supermarkets, storks bring babies, somebody picks up the trash, somebody cleans the windows, and somebody died for their sins. They never stop to think about it much, though. That's what keeps them passing by.

"Ready to go in?" said Rambam, getting up from the table.

"Go in where?"

"The Napoli i Roma Social Club, of course."

"Say what?"

"Think of it as visiting Chernobyl. It could be dangerous, but at least we'll probably be in and out quickly."

I got up a bit shakily and followed Rambam out the door of the little pastry shop. We stood on the corner and looked once more toward the major-crime-family-nerve-center-for-Manhattan that so blithely masqueraded as the Napoli i Roma Social Club. As the night had become darker, the place seemed to have taken on a rather deadly degree of darkness that was all its own. It could've been a store front. It could've been just another bar or coffee shop. It could've been merely a social club. But it wasn't. And it didn't want to be.

"One more thing," said Rambam. "If we do happen to run into Joe the Hyena, don't say: 'I'm Jewish. Can I call you Hy?' "

CHAPTER THIRTY-SIX

WE DIDN'T go into the gates of hell blindly. We didn't go in immediately either. Rambam made a brief pit stop at a corner souvenir shop and emerged wearing a late-model Mussolini T-shirt. Then he stopped at a nearby street vendor's cart and rounded out his outfit with a cheap straw cowboy hat to complement my own.

"Not bad for two bucks," he said.

"Except that it makes you look like a gay line dancer," I said.

"Better a live gay line dancer," said Rambam, "than a dead Joey Gallo."

"I'm not so sure of that," I said. "I have to agree with what Sandy Wolfmueller said when you tried on a cowboy hat in Pampell's Drug Store back in Kerrville, Texas. It's alarmingly anti-Semitic, of course, but nonetheless, her immortal words have forever been emblazoned upon my scrotum."

"I know," said Rambam with a sneer. " 'That cowboy hat makes your nose look big.' "

"That wasn't a bad Texas accent. Lose the falsetto, of course. This might just work."

"Of course it'll work. We're just two good ol' boys from Texas up here visiting the big city. In this outfit I should pass for a majorly obnoxious Texas tourist. Unfortunately, you've always looked and acted the part."

"But if we get in there what do we *do*? And do we really *want* to get in there?"

"Of course we want to get in there," said Rambam with some heat. "I thought we've been over this. We've only got two likely ways to go on this thing. Two real leads to follow. The fucking Indians and the fucking ex-wives. If we run them both down, I think we've got a good chance to crack this son of a bitch. But if you're not willing to follow the fucking leads you might as well stay home and play with your puppet head."

"His mother won't let him play after dark."

"As for the guys in the social club, just follow my lead. Lay the Texas hick number on them thick. They're bound to buy it. Believe me, these guys are not mavens of comparative culture."

"Hell," I said, "they probably wouldn't know culture if it kicked 'em in the ass."

"Which is probably what's going to happen to us as soon as I open this door," said Rambam.

Nevertheless, he did.

The first thing I saw was a large Italian flag and a large American flag hanging on a wall over several small tables, a few pinball machines, and a large, ornate espresso machine like the one in my loft. It made me wish I were back at my loft, possibly playing with my puppet head or talking to the bathroom mirror. There didn't seem to be anyone or anything moving in the place.

"Not exactly a killer-bee hive of activity," I murmured to Rambam.

"The maître d' must be off tonight," he said, as we walked warily into the room.

Other than Rambam and myself the only two faces I could see in the place belonged to the Pope and Fiorello La Guardia, and they both looked like they'd been there on the wall since Marconi ate his first macaroni. Fiorello was smiling. The Pope was not. Neither were me and Rambam.

"They're in the back somewhere," said Rambam. "We'll have to draw them out."

"Or we could just draw ourselves out."

But the time for that appeared to be over. Rambam was already getting into high gear with his Texas tourist routine.

"Lookee here, Billy Ray! They saved a table for us!"

"I just lost my appetite," I said, staring up at a neat row of sharp, gleaming meat hooks set high into the wall as a seriously macabre coatrack.

"Keep up the Texas bullshit," Rambam hissed. "Otherwise, *we'll* be the dead meat."

"Yee-hah," I said.

"Ol' Connie swears this is the best little Eye-talian restaurant in all of Neeeeewww York!" said Rambam, as he moved across to the table, scraped a chair back loudly, and sat down. I followed and took the chair across from him.

As we both sat in a ridiculous tableau at the small table, the thought occurred to me, and not for the first time, that Rambam had finally gone a Brooklyn Bridge too far and this time the mob, as it were, was coming with torches to burn it down behind us before we could scurry back to the mundane insanity that had been our lives. I'd followed Rambam into some dangerous places—a deadly warehouse in New Jersey, a former Nazi's brownstone, an FBI surveillance site, even a late-night bugging of a psychiatrist's office which, judging from the current situation, was exactly where we both belonged. Yet somehow Rambam had always managed to pull the rabbit out of the hat. Of course the hat had not been sitting on the head of the little old man who looked like a Carlo Gambino impersonator and was now coming out of the back room and shouting in a grizzled Italian accent.

"Luigi!" he yelled in the thick, staccato cadences of a fascist machine gun. "You-no-watch-a-the-fuckin-door?"

"That durned ol' Connie Nelson," Rambam continued obliviously. "She ain't never been wrong in a coon's age. Ol' Connie and Shirley say they give all their business to only this one little ol' Eye-talian restaurant. Said Joe would take care of us. Bring me a chili dog, buddy, will ya?"

"Luigi! Sal! Vinnie! Larry!" shouted the old man, as he turned toward the back of the place in disgust and fury.

"Larry?" said Rambam.

"Let's get out of here," I said, "before they have to wheel us on two gurneys down Mulberry Street."

"What the hell's the matter with you, Billy Ray? How often you get to little ol' Neeewww York? Are you Willie Nelson's nephew or ain't you? Answer me that, you autistic son of a bitch!"

Rambam delivered this last line staring me meaningfully in the eyes. He did not look the least bit flustered. The bastard had to be crazy. It seemed to me I only had two possible courses of action. Sit tight and tough it out, hoping Rambam remotely knew what he was doing, or bug out for the dugout yesterday. While I was busy weighing my options, a large curtain was flung open behind us to reveal another room. In it was a green felt gaming table where a couple of young guys in muscle shirts had apparently been playing cards. Now they were getting up from the table. They did not appear to be overly happy about the interruption of their game.

"Hell yes, I'm Willie Nelson's nephew!" I shouted. "I'm also Pavarotti's cousin!"

My ass seemed welded to the little wooden chair at

the moment but in my peripheral vision I picked up three or four guys moving menacingly toward us from the back room.

"Waiter!" Rambam shouted cheerfully. "Dago red!"

Now four pairs of dead eyes were converging on the small table. I'd seen several of these guys before, I thought, some years ago back in the loft. Maybe if they were carting an espresso machine through the door I could tell for sure. But of course they weren't. Now they wore muscle shirts and black silk tank tops, flashed lots of tattoos, and said not a word. In their eyes was nary a flicker of recognition, not to mention humanity. Only the old guy with the hat and Rambam were still doing any talking.

"You-fuckin-cowboy-tourists-you-getta-the-fuck-oud-dahere!" shouted the old man.

"I shore hope the food's better than the service," said Rambam, in the blithe tones of a village idiot. "Connie said Joe would take care of us—"

"I'll take care of you," said one of the young guys in a soft, yet eager, voice.

He grabbed two large handfuls of Rambam's Mussolini T-shirt and, as he pulled him up from the table, Rambam grabbed two large handfuls of his black silk tank top.

"Luigi!" shouted the old man. "You-no-watch-a-the-front-door?"

"I go away for a couple seconds," said Luigi with an expressive shrug.

Rambam and the guy were now waltzing around like two dancing bears, knocking over what little furniture there was in the place. More than anything the room looked like a friendly, traditional, Italian kitchen, except that it wasn't friendly and the only thing cooking was a big cauldron of trouble in extra-thick ugly sauce.

Just as one of the muscle shirts grabbed my arm and helicoptered me out the door, I saw the dancing bears

crash heavily into the Pope. By the time I picked myself
up out of the gutter, the doorframe seemed to have projec-
tile-vomited Rambam as well. The door closed, then
opened again as Luigi frisbeed Rambam's straw cowboy
hat onto the sidewalk.

"Fuckin'-Texas-tourists-stay-the-fuck-ouddahere!!"
we heard the old man shouting.

Then Luigi closed the door again and this time we
heard the bolt slide into place. Rambam was smiling as he
picked himself up off the street and then picked up his
straw cowboy hat off the sidewalk. He placed it firmly on
his head and we walked down Mulberry and across Canal
Street into Chinatown. We stopped at a window with some
roast ducks hanging in it and looked at our reflections for
a moment. Two Texas tourists gazed goofily back at us.

"Well," said Rambam, "the lead might've not panned
out, but at least I was right about one thing."

"What's that?"

"This cowboy hat makes my nose look big," he said.

CHAPTER THIRTY-SEVEN

SEVERAL DAYS later I was sitting at my desk one gloomy afternoon watching a spider, not an Australian redback fortunately, crawling cautiously across my framed painting of Father Damien, the little Belgian priest who died of leprosy on the island of Molokai in 1889. I didn't mind the spider. Neither did Father Damien. After all, spiders, like policemen, are our friends. Spider-killers are just as bad as cop-killers to certain weird kinds of Buddhists. They believe that if you kill a spider you kill your dreams.

"Now what could be more ridiculous than that?" I said to the cat.

The cat, of course, said nothing, but she continued to watch the spider along with me and I thought I detected a green, hungry look in her eye. The cat was not a Buddhist.

Unfortunately, my client was. So just keep in mind, if you ever decide to become an amateur private investigator and you find yourself sleuthing on behalf of a Red Headed Stranger from Blue Balls, Montana, he's not going to be a hell of a lot of help in the hard-facts department. Willie had told me that since he was a small child, his greatest talent, according to him, was not singing and song writing. It was "getting myself into trouble and then getting myself out again." I was very much afraid, however, with time ticking down toward the big New York shows at Radio City Music Hall, and nothing of substance turning up on my end of things, that Willie might finally find himself failing at what he considered his greatest talent.

"I'm afraid," I said to the cat, "that Willie Nelson will never get out of this world alive."

The cat, of course, did not respond. She wouldn't've recognized a line from a Hank Williams song if somebody'd laid it out on a mirror for her. In truth, the sad fact was that the cat had never been a fan of country music. If she had been, however, she'd probably listen to Garth Brooks, whom I sometimes refer to as The Anti-Hank. One of those guys who represented the new breed of what they now called country music. The only thing any of them have in common is that they've all grown up listening to Dan Fogelberg. Many of them had hated the sounds of Hank Williams and Willie Nelson when they were younger and they'd probably never worn a hat until their record producer, who'd just moved to Nashville from L.A., had put one on top of their head, which, no doubt, contained a brain about the size of a small Welsh mining town. One of the few "new country" singers I liked today was Lee Roy Parnell, who claimed to have been a "teenage Jewboy" and, in fact, had played in my band, the Texas Jewboys, for several years, back when Willie was divorcing his eighty-seventh wife. Lee Roy was a real talent, had paid his dues with interest, had been married almost as many times as Willie, and, much to his credit in these trendier-than-thou days, he never wore a hat.

I looked at Father Damien's picture again. He'd been wearing his hat for a long, long time. It was a rather weatherbeaten liturgical number, held up on the sides by two frazzled pieces of string. Damien, of course, was a rather weatherbeaten liturgical number himself, held up solely, and certainly souly, by his love of Jesus. Not the Jesus of the Crusades. Not the Jesus of the Inquisition. Damien loved Jesus the carpenter. Jesus the embracer of lepers. Jesus the guy who died trying.

Indeed, Damien was one of the most Christ-like human beings to travel down the old lost highway in a while. He, too, was a carpenter, and he built the Church of St. Philomena on Molokai. St. Philomena is the patron saint of hopeless causes, which, as we all know, are the only ones really worth fighting for. Damien, like Jesus, embraced the lepers and considered himself one of them, which in time, of course, he truly became in body and spirit. In 1873, when Damien first arrived on Molokai, he was thirty-three years old, Jesus's age at death, and he vaguely resembled a Belgian James Dean. Sixteen years later when he died, he looked like the Hunchback of New York. He arrived in the midst of a human hell, where doctors left their prescriptions on fence posts so as not to get near their patients, where fellow priests, officials, and occasional visiting dignitaries were invariably moved to tears, almost none of them ever coming back again, where, in order to come up with ten fingers at the church organ, two players were needed, where no one could enter and no one could leave except through the bone orchard where thousands of his brothers and sisters were buried and Damien finally in order to make confession rowed out to meet a priest on a passing ship, and, when not allowed to board, shouted his personal torment up to the priest from his small boat in what has become known as Damien's confession at sea, where, joined later by the ever-loyal Brother Joseph Dutton and calm spirit of Mother Marianne, he did what he could to soothe the pain, elevate the spirit, build the coffins, dig the graves, and recite the final blessings over those who had found Jesus as Jesus had found them. Like Jesus, Damien was at odds with the attitudes and the church of his day, and today, over a hundred years later, Damien's sainthood is still waiting in the wings, the infallible Pope falling in the bathtub and breaking his leg in 1994, thereby further delaying Damien's beatification. The other minor problem for the church was that Damien, apparently, had performed no miracles, other than, of course, laying down his life for his friends, which is a rare enough event to be considered a miracle in any man's book.

Scarcely a week before Damien's death, though in great physical pain and anguish, and running out of time to reach his wretched flock, he was seen atop the roof of St. Philomena's Church, shouting instructions to carpenters, and driving like hell in his horse and cart, taking short cuts across the Protestant cemetery.

On his deathbed he reported to Brother Dutton that he could see two figures, one standing at the head and one standing at the foot of the bed. Damien appeared to know who they were, but he never told Dutton. After Damien's martyrdom, thousands of letters came pouring in to Brother Dutton from around the world asking if the sender might come to Molokai to help at the colony. Brother Dutton dutifully answered them all, kindly declining their requests. "You can find your Molokai anywhere," he told them.

"No shit," I said to the cat, as we watched the spider crawl across Damien's ravaged face and onto the koa wood frame of the painting. Damien didn't flinch. Just stood there in his tattered tunic and his old hat held up by the strings, holding a cross and staring out to sea through his little round John Lennon glasses as the mists of Molokai gently fell upon him and his chosen people.

"Part of me is Damien," I said to the cat, "and part of me is that spider."

CHAPTER THIRTY-EIGHT

THE DAYS crawled by until one lazy morning, little more than a week before Willie's first night at Radio City, I found myself at my desk watching a gray tendril of smoke climbing slowly to the ceiling and I thought once again of spiders. It occurred to me that Ariadne had placed two distinct threads of yarn in my hand and still I was wandering lost in the maze. Who was Ariadne? If you're not a student of Greek mythology you may well think she was a former girlfriend of mine. Quite possibly she was and at the time I was just too tied up to notice. But the Ariadne I'm speaking of was a young girl who may or may not have lived and died thousands of years ago, depending on whether or not you believe in Greek mythology, pointing the bone, Peter Pan, and the smudging of people's cats at four o'clock in the morning. I first came upon Ariadne, not sexually, at the University of Texas many years ago in a course of study called Plan II. Plan II is a highly advanced liberal arts program mainly distinguished by the fact that every student in the program has some form or other of facial tic.

Facial tics, of course, are not to be confused with spiders and ticks, which belong to the genre arachnid, which was named after Arachne, who challenged the goddess Athena to a weaving contest. But the genre arachnid could've just as easily been named after Ariadne, who led Theseus out of the labyrinth. Ariadne was the daughter of

Minos, the king of Crete for whom cretins were named, the king of Crete being pretty slow out of the chute himself in that he'd commanded King Aegeus to sacrifice a certain number of young men from Athens every year to a fierce creature called the Minotaur who was half man and half bull and lived in a labyrinth. If you went into the labyrinth, even if the Minotaur didn't kill you, you never came out of there again. You had to spend the rest of your life listening to a guy sing Jimmy Buffett cover songs.

Finally, just as the King of Crete was starting to really get up the sleeve of King Aegeus's robe or toga or whatever was fashionable back then, Aegeus's own son, Theseus, volunteered to enter the maze and try to slay the Minotaur, thus interrupting what might have been a highly lucrative career in urology.

To put the myth on a bumper sticker, Ariadne slipped Theseus a dagger and a spool of gold thread which he tied to a rock at the entrance of the labyrinth and unraveled as he went along until he came upon, not sexually, by the way, the monstrous half-man half-bull Minotaur and started to come unraveled himself. But Theseus threw dirt in the Minotaur's eyes, stabbed it three times in the heart, cut off its head, and followed Ariadne's golden thread out of the labyrinth to safety.

With Ariadne in tow, Theseus then set sail for Athens on his way to becoming one of the greatest heroes in Greek mythology. Unfortunately, through an error on the part of the Cretan captain, who was definitely a cretin, the ship sailed into Athens with black sails instead of white, thereby wrongly signaling to King Aegeus that his son Theseus had stepped on a rainbow and gone to Zeus. The good king thereupon performed a grief-stricken swan dive into the sea which now bears his name.

All of this, of course, raises the question of whether or not it's always worthwhile to seek out and destroy the

Minotaurs of our lives. You may get the girl if you're successful, but you also may lose a loving father, and gain a
somewhat tedious father-in-law, not to mention giving up
what might have been a highly lucrative career in urology.
This, indeed, is one of the problems with mythology. It
seduces you, blends into your life, obscures reality, and
soon you no longer know if you're merely a mortal man or
a hero hefting a severed bull's head out of a labyrinth or,
as you're probably beginning to suspect, everything is just
bullshit.

As far as the twin threads of the Willie Nelson case
were concerned, I'd followed one of them about as far as
I intended to go and the other one still remained little
more than a dark smudge on a crimson horizon. Using the
word "smudge" advisedly. Or so I thought as I lit my first
cigar of the day and waited for the espresso machine to
finish humming an interminable version of the theme
from *Chariots of Fire.* As I recall, that was, as Rapid Robert might say, "about the time the doorknob broke." I'd
been sleepwalking through the investigation thus far and
now I was standing on the precipice about to be flung into
the Aegean Sea out of which all nightmares evolve.

It was the blower on the left that caused the trouble
this time. I hoisted it on the second ring and blew a cool
column of smoke toward the Isle of Lesbos.

"Start talkin'," I said.

The voice on the other end of the blower was soft,
familiar, troubled, road-weary. It belonged to Robby Romero.

"Kinky," he said. "This is going to kill you."

CHAPTER THIRTY-NINE

I WASN'T AFRAID of death. I just didn't want to die before the Willie Nelson concert in New York. Things had been moving along at a spider's pace lately but a heavy sense of fey was swirling about the loft along with the occasional wisps of residual cigar smoke. Willie hadn't been out on the road for almost two weeks and, almost as counterpoint, I hadn't been out on the street. Deep in my bones I felt that something was about to happen and the way things had been going whatever it was I sure as hell planned to take it and run with it.

"There's worse things than death, Robby," I said, "and one of them is waiting around for someone to tell you what it is that's going to kill you."

"It's the medicine bundle, Kinky."

"The thing we smudged the other night?"

"That's right. It's called a medicine bundle. In fact, it *is* a medicine bundle. In fact, it's not just *any* old medicine bundle."

"Well, what the hell is it, Robby? The goddamn Holy Grail?"

"The Holy Grail's only significant for a person if he's a Christian. I'm not a Christian and you weren't either the last time I checked."

"I'm a Jehovah's Bystander," I said. "We believe in a supreme being but we just don't want to get involved."

"I'm not sure you have a choice anymore," said

Robby. "I told you 'Tadodaho' is the fire-keeper—the one who preserves the history of the people. If anyone would know the authenticity of a medicine bundle it'd be 'Tadodaho' and his tribal elders. They didn't tell me and Benito a hell of a lot, but when we presented them with the bundle and they saw the contents it might as well have been dynamite from their reactions. Benito and I fell under immediate scrutiny. They wanted to know where we'd gotten it."

"That was the first thing you asked me after you leaped sideways out of the rocking chair."

"But I didn't question you for three entire days. We've been through a whole inquisition by almost every tribal elder and these were some serious, heavy dudes. Are you getting the picture, Kimosabe?"

"Okay, so they became highly agitato about the medicine bundle, but why didn't you get back to me sooner?"

"Because these guys run on Indian Standard Time and they wouldn't let us go. I'm telling you, Kinky, somebody's laid some heavy-duty shit on Willie this time and it ain't the kind you smoke."

I leaned back in my chair and looked out through the kitchen window at the cold, gray Manhattan morning that seemed to be turning colder and grayer by the minute. We'd bought the island from the Indians once for twenty-six beads and as I listened to garbage trucks grumble and watched fire escapes rust and pigeons shit and empty-eyed people scurry around like worried rats searching for their breakfast in garbage cans, I reflected, and not for the first time, that we'd gotten hosed on the deal. I wasn't exactly sure yet who was behind this current round of chicanery but I damned sure didn't want to get burned by the Indians a second time.

"You still there, Kinky?"

"Where else would I be?"

"Benito's got something he'd like to tell you. Maybe you ought to hear him out. He's going to be a wise old tribal elder himself some day, you know."

"I'm not sure I can wait that long."

I heard the sounds of Robby exiting a phone booth and Benito coming in, along with a rush of background highway white noise.

"Where're you guys calling from, Benito?"

"Upstate. Just outside some big tourist-trap restaurant and gift shop with an Indian name."

"Two-Dogs-Fucking?" I said. "I think I know the place."

If Benito laughed at all I lost it in the highway noise. When he spoke again, his tone seemed almost somber.

"I have a theory about why the fire-keeper and the elders appear to be so—"

"Wrapped up in this bundle?"

"—Yeah. You could say that. I wouldn't but you could. You see, there's an old story—the Legend of Bluejacket—about Chief Tecumseh of the Shawnee, who got all the tribes together to fight the last serious effort against the white man. This was in the Ohio Territory in the mid-nineteenth century. There was an American cavalryman called Bluejacket, who was Tecumseh's friend and fought alongside the Indians. The chief thought that Bluejacket might be able to convince other white men of the injustice that had been wreaked upon the Indians and possibly be the conduit to peace before it was too late. Tecumseh is said to have given Bluejacket a medicine bundle as a token of peace and brotherhood and goodwill. Of course, peace and brotherhood and goodwill never happened. Only death and destruction followed in the wake of this medicine bundle. The point is, the Iroquois believe what you gave to us the other night is Bluejacket's medicine bundle."

"Jesus Wing Fat," I said.

"So you see it is old, sacred, powerful medicine that's been stolen and lost to us for many years and now, because of what happened in Arizona, it's come back up here to the fire-keeper. The Iroquois, incidentally, often shared medicine with the Shawnee. By the way, Kinky, the guy who was hit on the highway in Arizona was a Hopi. It's not their way to pursue revenge or destruction, so they would never use this medicine even though all the tribes, of course, have total faith in its power. If there was a way to stop the medicine we would. But what Robby told you before is right, Kinky. There's nothing anyone can do now."

Benito spoke these words with such sincerity and quiet authority that I almost believed them myself. Almost. When you live in the white man's world, of course, there's no "total faith" in anything. I puffed on the cigar for a moment, silently absorbing Benito's little history lesson. So the long-lost medicine bundle had turned up in a most unexpected way. Years ago it had been given by an Indian to a white man. Shaken loose by the Arizona incident, it had now been returned to its people. But not by the Hopi, who had always walked the path of peace. And all the tribes had total faith in the power of the bundle. At last I could feel my mind beginning to follow the thread through the labyrinth. It was starting to make sense now. Whoever was going after Willie Nelson *had to be a white man*. And I was pretty damn sure where to start looking for him.

"By the way, Benito," I said, "whatever happened to Bluejacket?"

"He died," said Benito. "Like everyone else in the story."

CHAPTER FORTY

BLOWER TRAFFIC was heavy into and out of the loft that afternoon. Doug Holloway had intercepted and read to me several rambling, vaguely threatening, typewritten letters that had been sent to Willie within the past week. They served to confirm several points that had already been worrying me.

"Any postmarks?" I said, when Doug had finished reading both letters over the blower.

"Nada," said Doug. "But our boy does appear to have a pretty good sense of humor."

"Yeah," I said. "The line about 'Sorry I missed you in Buffalo' was a real killer."

"So was the bit about 'Be careful in New York—I hear there's a lot of crime up there.'"

"And they're both signed 'The Green Arrow'?"

"That's right, Kinky," said Doug, in a voice a children's show host on television might use when addressing a puppet.

"And Willie's off the road until New York?"

"That's right, Kinky."

"Would Willie consider canceling the New York shows until we get a better handle on this guy?"

"You know the answer to that. If the whole Sioux Nation rose up against him and came galloping down Broadway he'd still be up there at the microphone singing 'Whisky River.' Threats and intimidation never work with Willie."

"Neither does common sense."

"That's right, Kinky," said Doug, who was beginning to get up my sleeve with what I felt was an uncalled for surplus of That's right, Kinky's.

Willie had stubborn staked out. When Doug had showed him the two letters, he'd merely laughed them off. "Just don't put him on the guest list," he'd said.

"If I only had a little more time," I said, "I'm sure I could run this guy down. I know he had to have been in Arizona around the time and place of the bus accident. I also know, in spite of everything to the contrary that he's a white man."

"Why couldn't the guy have just read about the accident or heard about it somewhere?"

"Not likely. The incident never went beyond the Honeysuckle Rose for a good long while. Even you didn't know about it and you're so close to Willie that when he eats the watermelon you spit out the seeds. Usually at me, I might add."

"Flattering job description like that won't get you anywhere, Kinky. And by the way, how can you be so sure it's not what it looks like? The bus happened to flatten an Indian and some friend or relative or small group of tribal troublemakers got into the firewater and went on the warpath against Willie. What's wrong with that scenario?"

"Well, it's factually, not to mention politically, incorrect."

"Knowing how important being politically correct has always been to you I'm suddenly overcome with shame at my insensitivity."

"Every Indian is not a drunk," I continued stolidly.

"I'm sure that's true," said Doug. "I just want to know when you turned in your ten-gallon yamaha, resigned from the kosher cowboys, and joined up with the American Indian Movement."

My mind went back to the week before. It was very late at night in the loft and the smell of sage filled the air. Eagle feathers brushed my shoulders like forgiving wings of angels I never knew I had. I could hear Robby and Benito softly chanting in the background in a language never required, never taught in college. I thought of Benito speaking to me from a roadside pay phone near Poughkeepsie about the legend of Bluejacket, the white man who befriended and fought alongside Tecumseh against his own people. The first great white hope that never happened. I looked at the eyes of the cat and saw strange fires burning there. Possibly the reflection of the red-hot tip of my cigar as I puffed and peered almost hypnotically at the little red fires burning inside rounded fields of green then yellow then green like a living traffic light. Maybe little Indians were burning sage in there or little Jews were burning candles. Quite possibly little Germans were burning books or little rednecks were burning black churches or little blacks were burning Korean grocery stores. They were really settin' the woods on fire and yet the cat just sat there stoically staring at me with the slightly quizzical gaze of a New Age businessman. I thought of something Carl Jung had once observed when he wasn't busy giving himself a checkup from the neck up. He'd said: "We meet ourselves time and time again in a thousand disguises on the path of life."

I'd pretty much forgotten what Doug's question had been, so I puffed on my cigar and tried to come up with what might pass for a mildly metaphysical, spiritually ubiquitous answer.

"Many moons ago," I said.

Doug seemed to accept this answer, but still I knew he wanted more. Like Kawliga the cigar-store Indian, I sat at my desk and waited.

"Okay," said Doug, "but why do you insist there has

to be a white man behind all this? Remember, Ben claims to have seen an Indian just before he got shot."

"Could've been one of the thousand disguises," I said. "The point is it's something we all should've known if we hadn't been ignorant of the significance of the medicine bundle the Indian gave Willie in Florida—"

"There you go. An Indian again."

"That one I believe was a rent-an-Indian hired specifically to deliver the medicine bundle to Willie. Either that or a disguise again—"

"Or the guy behind all this is an Indian—"

"No. That's the one point upon which I'd bet my life, such as it is. The bundle Willie received is very powerful medicine to the Indians, one and all. They believe the recipient will die a slow and painful death and there's absolutely nothing anyone can do about it. Receiving that bundle to them is comparable to your doctor telling you that you have AIDS or inoperable cancer."

"So?"

"Don't you see? If an Indian were behind this, he'd know that. There'd be no need to take a potshot at a guy in Buffalo who looks like Willie. There'd be no need to write threatening letters. The white guy gained possession of this bundle but he doesn't truly believe in its power. Any Indian certainly would."

"So I'll tell L.G. to alert his beefed-up security team to look for a white man, just possibly dressed as an Indian."

"I doubt it. I think he's run that gambit as far as it'll go. He won't try the same thing again. Just have them look out for a white man. Unless, of course, I find him first."

"Or unless Just Bill finds him. I forgot to tell you he left yesterday for Arizona to do some sleuthing around himself."

"Just Bill's in Arizona?"

"That's right, Kinky."

"That could be dangerous."

"For Just Bill or for Arizona?"

"Listen, Doug, this could be serious. Is there any way to reach him?"

"No, Chief Thundercloud, but if he calls I'll have him get in touch with you right away. And now I see Mr. Nelson himself coming and we have something to do that's even more important than life and death."

"Play golf?"

"That's right, Kinky."

CHAPTER FORTY-ONE

THERE WERE a great many white men in North America, and given that I did not know, or indeed wish to know, their various sexual proclivities, it was not going to be easy to determine who did and who didn't have a hard-on for Willie Nelson. Frankly, as the moments ticked ever closer to Willie's New York shows and I had time to consider the veneer of confidence I'd just finished laying on Doug Holloway, that, too, began to wane. Did I really know for sure that the guy was a white man? What if he was an Indian disguising himself as a white man disguising himself as an Indian? It wasn't bloody likely, of course, but it was a possibility. And until the possible truly became the impossible, the great detective himself would hardly let it fall from his talonlike grip into the gaslit gutters of London. I looked deep into the Delphian depths of Sherlock's porcelain eyes.

"Ah, Mr. Holmes," I said, "it seems quite hopeless. The fabric of reality is far too flimsy to support serious deductive reasoning in this highly singular case. In the past there's always been a shard, a scintilla, a shadow out of place to catch my weary eye and lead me to the light of truth. Here I have nothing. Nothing but a white man in a white man's world. I beseech you, Almighty Holmes, help me to find him in time."

I was, of course, laying it on pretty thick. Holmes had always been the court of last resort, however, and my little

problem was nothing new to him. Despair and hope-
lessness had always been drawn inexorably to the Statue
of Liberty–like lights that were his eyes. Now, as then, he
did not blink. All cold, pale porcelain bathing the modern,
mixed-up world in silence and science and strength.

I had to follow the Ariadne thread I was currently
clutching. You never change threads in the middle of the
labyrinth. Following it backward, the thread almost certainly began with what happened to the Honeysuckle
Rose. With someone who knew what happened soon after
it had happened. A white man. In Arizona. But I wasn't
the only Theseus of the Interstate, I thought uncomfort-
ably. I wasn't the only amateur who thought of himself as
a detective. Nor was I the only mortal who wanted to be a
hero. Ariadne, apparently, had led Just Bill to Arizona
ahead of me.

With what seemed like somewhat of a second wind,
spiritually speaking, I picked up the blower on the left and
called Mark Rothbaum's office in Connecticut. This time,
rather miraculously, I got through.

"Sorry, Kinkster," he said, "but I've been in Europe
with another artist."

"Don't tell me Modigliani's going out on the road
again."

"Another artist," of course, meant anyone else besides Willie, whom Mark had managed for many years. In
total fairness to the man, he'd also managed, at one time
or another, such names as Miles Davis, Emmylou Harris,
Roger Miller, and Don Imus's second-favorite singer, Del-
bert McClinton. All great artists, I figured, had to be dead
or else they quite often wished that they were. That's what
made them so hard to manage.

"I take it you're calling about Willie," said Rothbaum.
"This Indian business."

"Correctimundo."

"I'm worried about it, too, Kinkster. How can I help you?"

"Willie tells you lots of things in confidence. I may need to know some of them now. Like the accident with the Honeysuckle Rose. Exactly where it took place."

"They were on Interstate Forty heading for a gig in Laughlin, Nevada. As near as I can pinpoint it—which I can't do very precisely—it happened about a hundred miles or so from the New Mexico border. Willie said it was about an hour and a half after they crossed into Arizona. Willie's really worried about this, Kinkster, though he doesn't like to talk about it. He can't believe the Indians would fuck with him like this."

"I can't either. Let's go back even further than the bus incident. You had some weird theories about Willie's problems with the government?"

"I'm not a conspiracy freak, but it is possible that one hand of the government washes the other sometimes. I'm not saying the IRS trouble was in any way related to the earlier flap with the FBI, but—"

"Mark, what are you talking about?"

"Why, the concert for Leonard Peltier, of course. Back in the fall of eighty-five."

Robby had mentioned Peltier to me, but it hadn't really registered. My mother had stepped on a rainbow in May of that year and by October I was touring Australia with the Four Horsemen: my father, Earl Buckelew, and Mike McGovern, not to mention myself, because I wasn't really all there at the time. I dimly remember being on a yacht on the Great Barrier Reef as guests of Piers and Suzanne Akerman, both of whom were superb sailors and both of whom continually squabbled over who was the captain. I woke up aboard the boat on my forty-second birthday with the kookaburras laughing in the trees, still not believing that my mother had gone to Jesus or the

Southern Cross or wherever all our mothers go, but at least taking comfort in the knowledge that I was still my mother's son. Nowhere in my consciousness was a man named Leonard Peltier.

"Tell me about the concert," I said.

"Well, it was a benefit for Peltier, whom the Indians claimed was innocent but whom the feds and law enforcement regarded somewhat differently and tried to frame him for the deaths of two FBI agents. Cowboys love Indians, you know. Country artists have always felt the Indians got shafted and Willie is, of course, no exception. The concert got off on an interesting note with the feds crawling all over the place and Robin Williams getting on stage and shouting: 'Fuck the FBI!' "

"That must've been a crowd-pleaser."

"Oh, it was. Of course, most of Willie's guys were scurrying back to the buses to hide the dope. Kristofferson was on the show, too. The point is that everyone knew Robin Williams was a comedian and that Kris was a commie, but as far as the rednecks were concerned, Willie was theirs. When he got up there, they felt betrayed. Word got out that he'd done a benefit for a cop-killer and as late as the summer of eighty-six there were still four hundred cops picketing a show in Providence, Rhode Island."

"Fuck 'em if they can't take a joke."

"That's what Willie said. But the fact was that from the FBI to the Fraternal Order of Police to local law enforcement around the country there was some very deep-seated, hate-filled anti-Willie sentiment swirling around. Finally, Willie had to call William Sessions, then director of the FBI, and get him to make his boys lay off. There hasn't really been any trouble since that time. Now it's all pretty much ancient history. Is there anything else? I've got to run."

"No. You've been very helpful, Mark. I know you're busy—"

"No. I'm not *busy*. I've just literally got to *run*. I'm not a conspiracy freak but I probably could be called a fitness freak. I've even developed a machine that measures my resting heartbeat when I first wake up in the morning."

"Mark, that may be a little more than I need to know about your personal life—"

"My waking heart rate, by the way, is forty-two. Of course, if I speak to Willie in the morning it shoots up to about a hundred and forty."

"That must give you a nice little rush. One more thing, Mark."

"Fire away."

"Where's Leonard Peltier today?"

"Still in Leavenworth," he said.

CHAPTER FORTY-TWO

I CRADLED the blower only for about the time it takes a country singer's heart to break. Then I quickly collared it again and called the top-secret number on Willie's bus. I have found that whether Willie's out on the road or home in Texas loitering around the golf course, the Honeysuckle Rose is the home he never really leaves for long. It was ironic, indeed, that it should now be the very vehicle through which disaster might have finally found him.

Willie, as I well knew, was playing golf, a passion of his possibly only matched by O.J. Simpson's passion for golf. I once asked Willie, since both men were bonded by love of golf, if O.J. were to walk up to him, would he shake hands with the man? "I'd shake hands with him," said Willie, "but I wouldn't let him ride on the bus."

In my opinion, of course, O.J. was punished enough when they revoked his membership card to Hooters. That kind of cruel cut is something from which a man seldom comes back. One of the only guys I know who actually was a friend of O.J.'s is Bud Shrake, who's been a sportswriter for many years and once made the eyewitness locker-room observation that O.J. had the second-largest penis in all of sports. The only larger penis, according to Shrake, who, like the rest of us, can sometimes be a fairly large penis himself, belongs to Cesar Cedeno, the baseball player who, incidentally, stabbed his wife to death. This doesn't mean that anyone with a larger-than-life penis is predestined to stab his wife to death. It just means that some of us should be a little more careful. Further study and gathering of data are, of course, required. I asked Shrake if he would indeed be interested in working with me on such a project, but he demurred. I asked Willie if he'd be interested in the project but he also declined. He did, however, come up with a rather insightful corollary to the theory. "When it's too short," said Willie, *"they* stab *you."*

Since neither Willie nor O.J. were on the bus, and there was very little likelihood that O.J. would ever be on the bus, I had to make do with L.G. and Gator, the size of whose penises was not really germane to the investigation, but whose presence suited my purposes perfectly. All dicking around aside, the investigation suddenly seemed to be shuddering toward a somewhat surprising climax. I realized now, as I probably should've long before, that the precise pinpointing of the site of the bus accident was crucial to the solution I sought. Law enforcement personnel are known to be extremely territorial animals. L.G. and Gator had probably unknowingly held the key to the case the whole time. As we spoke now, I felt that key irrevocably changing hands.

"Kinky wants to know *exactly where* you ran into that drunken Indian and collected ten points," shouted L.G.

"Still not funny," I could hear Gator shout back.

"Every Indian is not a drunk, L.G.," I said.

"I know," said L.G. "That's why he collects ten points. Near as I can remember it happened about twenty miles west of Winslow on Interstate Forty—"

"Exactly thirteen miles west of Winslow," shouted Gator in the background. "It's not the kind of thing you're ever likely to forget."

"One last item, L.G.," I said. "The law-enforcement guys who investigated the accident. Who were they?"

"Big ol' state troopers with big ol' guns. Looked like they just rode out of the Old West."

"Just Bill said there were also sheriff's deputies."

"Just Bill's crazy as a bedbug besides not having been there. There were no deputies at the scene, only state troopers. And there were six of them, all from the substation outside of Winslow that covers all of Navajo County, Arizona. I know because I talked to every goddamn one of them."

"Remember any names?"

"Hell, no. You meet a lot of state troopers when you work with Willie."

"I'll bet you do. Look, L.G., if you should hear from Just Bill, please have him call me right away. He's mucking around out there in Arizona and it could be very dangerous."

"It could be very dangerous mucking around right out here," said L.G. "You could get hit by a golf ball."

"Well, thanks, L.G. You've been very helpful. And thank Gator for me."

"Best not. This conversation's already workin' on his last t-cell. No matter what you tell him, he still seems to feel he was somehow to blame."

"It wasn't his fault. If anybody's to blame, it's Ariadne."

"Sounds familiar. Wasn't she the tall blonde with the nice set of honkers?"

"No," I said. "That was Helen of Troy, New York."

CHAPTER FORTY-THREE

THE ONLY GUY who ever solved mysteries sitting on his large Montenegran buttocks was Nero Wolfe, and though I knew I wasn't him I also knew that Arizona was a long way from Vandam Street. Besides, we already had one man too many in the field right now. That was Just Bill. If I didn't miss my bet, the guy who arranged to have the medicine bundle sent to Willie, dressed up like an Indian and shot Ben Dorsey, and then sent Willie troublingly humorous threat notes was a very dangerous animal indeed. Prison personnel will tell you that murderers, when discussing their evil deeds, will invariably crack wise, often revealing a good, if sick, sense of humor, laughing and chuckling to no one in particular when they get to the gruesome parts. The guy we were looking for was hellbent to make somebody die laughing and I didn't want that somebody to be Willie Nelson. I hopped back on the blower in the time it takes a cockroach to circumnavigate a puppet head.

"Even the hard-boiled computer has to have something for breakfast every now and then," said Rambam. "You've got to provide me the names of those six Arizona state troopers."

"How the hell would I know their names?" I said. "L.G.'s the one who talked to them and *he* doesn't even remember their names."

"Try the old Lost Speeding Ticket Gambit."

"The old Lost Speeding Ticket Gambit! That's a wonderful idea. What is the old Lost Speeding Ticket Gambit?"

"Call the fucking substation near Winslow. Tell 'em you were driving through a while back, and you got a speeding ticket which you've inadvertently misplaced but if they tell you the officers' names it might jog your memory. You want to be a good citizen. Just sound sincere and you can't miss."

"How the hell am I going to sound sincere?"

"To quote Kinky Friedman: 'Sincerity is very important in this business. Once you learn to fake that, you can do just about anything.' "

I cradled the blower on Rambam and got to work digging up the number of the state troopers substation in the Winslow area. The instructions were more difficult than they seemed on the seed packet, and I was fairly sure the results were not going to be as pretty. I had to find out if there was a transplanted Easterner hiding somewhere in my little crop of Arizona state troopers all in a row. The stark facts that the medicine bundle emanated from this area, that the failed hit had occurred in Buffalo, New York, and that the next opportunity to cap Willie would be in New York City all were piling on top of each other and making me a little nervous in the service. Still, I persevered. After three espressos and two and half cigars, my efforts were rewarded by God, the Buddha, Allah, or L. Ron Hubbard, take your pick.

"State troopers. Navajo County," said a voice that sounded like it belonged to a narcoleptic Wyatt Earp impersonator.

"Hi there," I said. "This is Charlie Starkweather from up here in Nebraska. I was passin' down your way a few months ago and I got a speedin' ticket."

"Yessir."

"Anyways, I meant to pay it when I got home but you know how these things are. I got ready to pay it and it turns out I lost the little booger."

"Yessir."

"I don't recollect the exact amount but it's been botherin' my conscience lately and I want to take care of it. I also don't remember the name of the officer. Nice, clean-cut young fella."

"Yessir."

"I was hopin' maybe you could tell me the names of a few of the troopers who work out of your station and the name of the officer might jog my memory."

"Yessir. Just a moment."

The old Lost Speeding Ticket Gambit seemed to be moving along at a rapid clip. I puffed on the cigar and winked at the cat. The cat was asleep on the desk and did not respond.

"Was it Don Helms?"

"That doesn't sound right."

"Was it Bob McNett?"

"No. Wasn't him."

"Jerry Rivers?"

"I don't think so."

"Uh, how about Hiram Williams?"

"No. I'd've remembered that one. I've got an uncle named Hiram."

"How about Hillous Butrum?"

Hillous Buttocks was more like it, actually, but I wasn't complaining. The ploy did seem to be working. One more name and Charlie Starkweather could beat it back to hell.

"That's a possible," I said.

"Well, there's only one other officer who could've handled it. You're sure it was a state trooper that stopped you?"

"That's the only thing I *am* sure of."

"What about Arthur W. Upfield? Does that sound familiar?"

"That could be it. Let me just brew up a strong pot of decaf and go over these names again and I'll call you back when something clicks."

"Yessir."

Needless to say, I did not brew any decaf and I did not call him back. L.G. had put six state troopers at the scene of the accident and I now had their names. If Rambam was as good as his word, we could have our man very soon. If our man was an Arizona state trooper. And if this whole charade wasn't merely moldy Minotaur manure.

"Here's how it works," said Rambam, when I got him on the blower. "It's all done through social security numbers. Now, what're the first three digits of your number?"

"I'm not the guy we're looking for."

"I know that. Just give me the first three fucking digits."

"I'll give you one fucking digit."

"Look, do you want to see how us real detectives do this or not?"

"Okay," I said grudgingly. "Four-five-six."

"All right. Those numbers deal with place. Now give me the next two digits."

"Jesus. Why don't I just give you the whole damn number? Then you'll be able to know everything about me."

"I *already* know everything about you and, believe me, it isn't all very pleasant. I just need the next two digits. I want you to understand how we're going to be doing this."

"Seven-six," I said grimly.

"That's dealing with the date issued. Just sit back and relax a moment."

It was never easy to relax with Rambam. On the other hand, it was essential that I have his help at this seminal juncture. I puffed my cigar rather broodingly and waited. I didn't have to wait too long. In about twenty seconds he was speaking again.

"Your social security was issued in Texas in nineteen sixty-two," he said.

"Wow," I said admiringly, striving to keep the irritation out of my voice. Here we were in the eleventh hour of an investigation with a madman on the loose and I was stroking him on his computer technique. "How did you ever do that?"

"Magic," he said. "Now give me the fucking names of the six guys."

I gave Rambam the names. He said he'd call me back soon. I waited and puffed my cigar. The cat slept. Overhead the lesbian dance class kicked up its heels in sprightly fashion. The puppet head smiled. The pigeons fluttered just outside the windowsill. The garbage trucks grumbled. Somewhere in Brooklyn, Rambam was entering six names into his hard-boiled computer. Somewhere in Texas Willie Nelson was playing golf in the sunshine. Somewhere in Arizona, also in the sunshine, Just Bill was trying his hand at being a private dick. Or so I thought before the phones rang again.

After the call I walked over to the counter and shook hands with the bottle of Jameson. Bad news can sometimes make you want a drink. I poured a long shot into the old bull's horn and shoveled a toast to fallen comrades in the general direction of the darkening sky. I killed the shot as well as the notion that we were going to get out of this one relatively unscathed. With a dry-eyed, don't-give-a-damn countenance, I was studying that little birdless, kiteless, godless patch of New York sky over Vandam Street when, thankfully, the phones rang again.

"We've got our man," Rambam said excitedly. "Arthur W. Upfield. Born in fifty-four or fifty-five. Social security card issued in New York."

"Great."

"You don't sound overly thrilled."

"We're just a little too late for Just Bill," I said. "He was killed this morning in Arizona by a hit-and-run driver who I'm also fairly sure is our man. We're now going after a murderer."

"What was this Just Bill guy doing down there in the first place?"

"Trying his hand at investigating."

"Just like somebody else I could mention. Were there any eyewitnesses?"

"None. Doug Holloway said that several passersby reportedly had seen him earlier in the morning."

"What was he doing?"

"Just standing on a corner in Winslow, Arizona."

PART FIVE

MONKEY

"You never know what the monkey eat
until the monkey shit."

—LEON "SLIM" DODSON

CHAPTER FORTY-FOUR

THERE'S ALWAYS something exciting going on at Radio City Music Hall. Especially when Willie Nelson's onstage and Arthur W. Upfield, the man I knew had murdered Just Bill, the man I knew had shot Ben Dorsey, was lurking in the wings. He was wearing a New York state trooper's uniform and carried a gun in his holster bigger than Vermont. Rambam and I, with NYPD Detective Sergeants Cooperman and Fox grudgingly in tow, had spotted Upfield even before the lights had gone down. We were sure it was him because he was wearing his name tag on his uniform.

"He's a ballsy bastard," said Rambam. "Wearing his fucking name tag."

"He has no reason on earth to believe anybody's onto him," I said.

"Let's just hope he's our man."

"He's got to be. What else would he be doing here?"

"He might be a Willie Nelson fan," Cooperman interjected, "like about five thousand other people here."

"Or he might be legitimate security," said Fox, "like about five thousand other people here."

"No way he's legitimate security," said Rambam. "He's not even a New York state trooper anymore. I checked him out. He was drummed out ten years ago for some shady behavior, drifted down to Arizona, and joined the troopers there. Like a priest that keeps buggering altar boys, when things got too hot he merely changed his locus."

"We're running our own check on him now," said Cooperman. "Unless he makes a move, nobody touches him until we get our results."

"Let's hope you don't get them too late," I said.

I looked at Upfield out of the corner of my eye. A cool customer if I ever saw one, tapping his foot to "Whiskey River," with a tight little smirk on his face. Rambam had the shell casing in his pocket and that, unfortunately, was the only physical evidence we had. If it matched the shell casings Upfield carried with him, it might be enough. But everything else was circumstantial and that was a kind word for it. His origins in Iroquois country. His leaves of absence to Florida, very likely, and to Buffalo, very definitely. The hit-run of Just Bill tied in nicely with the general theme he'd chosen—revenge for the bus accident. His letters might possibly be traced to a typewriter in Arizona. And here he was in his old New York state trooper's uniform, thousands of miles from his new home, up here to catch a Willie Nelson concert. It was enough for me, but I doubted if it'd be enough for Cooperman.

"Look," I said to Cooperman, "we know he's no longer with the New York state troopers. Can't we just play it safe and have him arrested for impersonating an officer? I just don't like that look on his face."

"Maybe we'll just arrest you," said Fox, "for impersonating a private investigator. I never much liked the look on your face either."

"You're treadin' on thin ice, Tex," said Cooperman. "Your case against this bird looks pathetically fuckin' weak. Why don't you just let us keep an eye on him and you go home and talk things over with your cat."

"The cat's prejudiced," I said. "She hates uniforms."

"Thank Christ we're plainclothes," said Fox.

Willie weaved so seamlessly through his set he seemed not to care whether there were five thousand people out there, or a small group of old friends in a domino parlor, or no one at all but Willie and his old guitar playing for the silent stars and the man in the moon. That was part of his secret, I figured. He seemed not to care, yet all the while he did. I cared, too. I just didn't know what the hell I could do about it. The problem was that unless Upfield made his move, it was going to be hard to nail the bastard.

Cooperman and Fox, Rambam and myself, and L.G. and Willie's whole security team had been alerted to his presence, but I still didn't much like the odds and the stakes were about as high as they ever get in this world. Too high to let Upfield play his hand. Yet Cooperman was right. If we tried to take him down now there was nothing to hold him on but the hope that the shell casings matched. He most likely would squirm away and live to play another day. This was totally unacceptable to me. I couldn't allow this modern-day sword of Damocles to hang over Willie Nelson's dusty, dreamy cowboy head forever. Something had to be done tonight.

Willie sang. Upfield smirked. Cooperman and Fox conferred casually with each other. Finally, Rambam grabbed my arm and directed me to a dark corner of the backstage area. Cooperman and Fox didn't seem to notice. Neither did Upfield.

"Kinky," said Rambam with some intensity, "do you *really* believe this is the guy?"

"I *know* this is the guy."

"Then we have no choice. We've got to preempt the fucker."

"You may have noticed that he's larger than God," I said.

"No problem," said Rambam. "Our challenge will be to provoke him."

"Provoking people has never been very difficult for us in the past."

"And I've got an idea—"

"Sounds dangerous—"

"You know how these troopers, especially, like to think of themselves as macho men? They fucking hate faggots, as you Texans might say."

"Or they're alarmingly homophobic, as you New Yorkers might say."

"Anyway, if we can draw him into that men's room down the hall away from Fox and Cooperman's ever-watchful scrutiny, I may have a chance to beat the living truth out of him."

"Sounds good. How do we get him in there?"

"Well, you've often said that your personal goals are to be fat, famous, financially fixed, and a faggot by fifty-one. Here's your chance."

"You mean I'm supposed to impersonate a fagola and get him to follow me into the dumper?"

"Chase you into the dumper will be more like it, probably. Just get in touch with your feminine side a little bit and see what you can do. You're all we've got."

"Fuck me dead, mate. What do I say?"

" 'Fuck me dead, mate,' is not a bad start. You might want to go with the old standard 'Hi, big boy.' Just get him into the dumper without Cooperman and Fox and without tipping your hand about the case. You're very talented at irritating people. Do it now. I'll take care of the rest."

"Okay, but he sure looks like a mean fucker."

"You better hope not," said Rambam as he headed off toward the men's room with a little wave and an overly friendly smile.

There are some things in life you want to do and

there are some things in life that you have to do and what happened next clearly belongs in the latter category. As I carried out the action, I was again impressed with Rambam's accurate read on this character or possibly Rambam's more-than-passing knowledge of human nature. Of course, it helped that Cooperman and Fox, possibly drawn in by Willie's magic, had drifted away a bit and concentrated their vaunted scrutiny elsewhere. It also helped that this guy had a brain about the size of a small Welsh mining town. This alone, however, could not much ameliorate his low cunning or his lethal mentality. If anything, it made him all the more dangerous.

"Hi, big boy" caught him off his guard and some nice sensitive eye contact, followed by repeated brash references to his big gun and big nightstick had him glancing around furtively, then, sure enough, following me into the men's room.

Teaching a queer a lesson is something that very few big macho men can resist. This is because they fear all fagolas, fear all the people with the holes in the middle, fear that they secretly might be one or the other of them, fear their fathers, fear their mothers, fear their God, and fear that when they were growing up they might've mistakenly read too much Oscar Wilde. In Texas, of course, we consider anyone a queer who likes girls more than he likes football.

"Why you goddamn motherfuckin' queer," he said by way of Freudian introduction as he entered the men's room. I was standing seductively in the farthest corner of the place, trusting that Rambam, who had not as yet made his presence known, was waiting in one of the stalls.

"I'm gonna fuck you good," said Upfield, now beginning to relish the situation.

"Another dream come true," I said languidly.

The trooper came rushing toward me like a sentient,

overdue commuter train. I stood my ground and prayed to the ghost of Rock Hudson.

"Why you dirty, slow-leak, little fairy, I'll—"

That was as far as he got.

Like a sinewy shadow, Rambam struck suddenly from the second stall, grabbing Upfield's gun out of his holster and sending it crashing conveniently into a mirror very close to my head. The mirror splintered immediately and so did Upfield's composure.

"Seven years of bad luck," said Rambam.

"Who're you?" said Upfield, looking like someone had just hit him on the head with a hammer.

"I'm the Jewish Superman, you fuck!" shouted Rambam. "I'm going to tear your heart out!"

Before I could even grab the gun, Rambam had cartwheeled the big man into the stall and gone in right after him. I could've used a forklift to pick up Upfield's gun but once I had it in my hand I was faced with another predicament. If Upfield came out of that stall, it might be imperative for me to feed the monkey a few bullets. Father Damien and Jesus Christ and John Lennon and Nelson Mandela all might have to go to the back of the blue bus if Arthur Upfield stepped out of that toilet stall alone. I might have to join the legions of zealots and fools and heroes and assholes that throughout history have picked up a gun and killed a man. I had to admit I was ready spaghetti.

The bangings, thuddings, and cursings continued almost unabated inside the stall with no indication of who was on top, so to speak. Where in the hell, with all this racket, were Cooperman and Fox? I wondered. Where was Crazy Horse when you needed him? Finally, I heard a strange voice, imbued with that flat, frightening absence of humanity you sometimes hear when someone is speaking in tongues. It was Upfield.

"Well," said Upfield, "it wasn't Donny Fuckin' Osmond. It was *him* up there on that big stage . . . The Indian-lover who just *had* to help the cop-killer."

I lowered the gun with a trembling hand, just as Cooperman and Fox rushed into the place. Cooperman went for the stall and Fox came over to me.

"Would've come in sooner, Tex," he said. "We heard a lot of grunting in here, but we thought it was business as usual."

"Spare me the bathroom humor," I said.

"I'll take that gun now," said Fox. "I'll take you in, too, Tex. You're under arrest."

"Hold the weddin'," I said, as I handed over Upfield's gun to Fox. "What law could I have conceivably broken?"

"The Brady Bill," he said.

CHAPTER FORTY-FIVE

IT DID NOT especially make me feel proud to be an American when I thought of what I'd done to lure Arthur Upfield into the men's room. I guess you could call it simply an investigative technique. As I always say, whatever gets you through the investigation. There's probably a lot less difference than we think between homosexuals and heterosexuals, just as there's very little difference, if any, between the "criminal" and the "normal" mind. Whether we like it or not we're all part of one big soul. Or, as the seminal American folksinger Dave Van Ronk once told me: "Ballet is basketball for queers." Of course, I didn't like ballet and I didn't like basketball and I really didn't like the way Arthur Upfield was looking at me as we sat on either side of Rambam in the back of the plain-wrapped squad car.

Down at the cop shop things got sorted out. Slowly, tediously, sometimes rather unpleasantly, but, nonetheless, sorted out. The "confession" that Rambam had gotten out of Upfield by cartwheeling him across miles and miles of bathroom tiles and then banging his head repeatedly against the porcelain throne was ruled under duress. Cooperman and Fox, so they claimed, had not been privy to Upfield's utterances at the time. Nor did they probably realize that almost everything that ever happens on that throne could be ruled under duress. Elvis, Judy Garland, and Lenny Bruce died quite literally on that throne, the kind of ignominious mortal coda the Lord plays only for His brightest stars. Jim Morrison, it should be noted, was only allowed to find his eternal salvation in the tub.

None of this, of course, was discussed down at the cop shop. More mundane matters were the order of the day, or night, as the case may be. It's sometimes hard to tell when you spend a lot of time down at the cop shop. One thing became clear. Upfield was now not talking. Anything he'd happened to let slip before was now going to have to be sucked, fucked, or cajoled out of him by the more acceptable, conventional, civilized methods of the NYPD.

Nevertheless, it did not seem likely that Upfield would be attending any Willie Nelson concerts for a long, long time. Questions were being asked, background checks were being run, faxes were humming between New York and Arizona, shell-casing comparisons were getting under way as well as efforts to recover the bullet that had bit Ben Dorsey. Upfield wasn't going anywhere for a while. Unfortunately, so it seemed, neither were Rambam or myself.

Then finally, just as I was debating whether to end the ennui by impaling myself upon the tip of Fox's sharp tongue or jumping off the bridge of Cooperman's large nose, they let us go. In the early hours, Rambam and I walked the few blocks from the precinct house to the Monkey's Paw to pour a few drinks down our necks. We got in just as they were closing up and locking the door but Tommy the bartender kindly saw to it that we were locked in instead of locked out.

"Don't worry," said Rambam. "They'll nail Upfield. Once they get all that machinery in motion it's pretty certain they're going to come up with a strong case against him. They may even get him on that hit-and-run."

"Fine," I said. "Just as long as he's not dressed up in

Sitting Bull drag waiting for me when I get back to the loft."

We were both fairly exhausted, but we had a few rounds of celebratory drinks in honor of Upfield's impending incarceration and the successful conclusion of the case. We toasted good cops. We toasted bad cops. We toasted live cops. We toasted dead cops. We toasted undercover cops. We toasted rent-a-cops. We even toasted Cooperman and Fox. The only cops we didn't toast were feds, whom Rambam refused to drink to, and Arizona state troopers, whom I refused to drink to. Finally, we toasted Willie Nelson, who at the moment, no doubt, was probably back on the bus smoking a joint the size of Pier 17.

By the time we'd finished the last round we were both mildly amphibious. We stumbled out of the Monkey's Paw, I shook Rambam's paw, then I headed back across Seventh Avenue in the general direction of the cat. I felt a certain satisfaction, rare indeed in this business, about the way the case had wrapped up. I also felt an inner exhilaration and a sense of doing my damnedest to live out my dreams. Some of this was attributable, I reflected, to my having travelled and hung out with Willie Nelson and his family.

I thought of something Johnny Gimble, the great fiddle player, had told me on the bus on the way to one of Willie's gigs. He'd said that when he was a little boy he'd told his mother: "When I grow up I'm gonna be a musician." His mother had told him: "Make up your mind, son. You can't do both."

The little story not only applied to Johnny Gimble. It also applied to Willie Nelson and, if I had to make a wild guess, I'd have to admit it also applied to myself.

When I opened the door to my loft the place seemed darker than I'd remembered. As my eyes adjusted, I was shocked to see the shadowy figure of a man, backlit by a distant streetlamp, standing in the middle of my living room. He was smoking a cigar, and when the ashes burned hot, his eyes appeared, glittering slightly like cold obsidian.

It was not Arthur Upfield.

It was not the gypsy from the bathroom mirror.

"Who *are* you?" I said at last.

"Some people," he said, "call me Joe the Hyena."

CHAPTER FORTY-SIX

ARIADNE'S a funny old girl, all right. Sometimes she gives you a line and sometimes she merely hands you one. As far as Joe the Hyena went, I soon found out there was no string attached. Joe, it emerged, was a Willie fan, and had taken it as his sacred duty to God and country music to square some old gambling debts run up by several of Willie's exes some years ago in Atlantic City. He also offered to help the Kinkster if I was ever in similar circumstances and some of the boys were trying to put the squeeze on me. We sat at the kitchen table for a while, chatting amiably, smoking cigars, and finally, knocking back a few espressos together.

"This old baby still delivers," he said, standing by the espresso machine and patting it lightly, for it was quite hot, apparently, in more ways than one.

"It's killer bee," I said. "Can't thank you enough for it."

"Forget it. You know who this espresso machine used to belong to?"

"Who?"

"It's better you don't know. Look, I got to go. Got to do some business tonight."

"In Little Italy?"

"It's better you don't know. But, hey, if you ever need me, you know where to find me."

"The social club?"

"Yeah. By the way, I'll try and see that the boys are a little more sociable next time."

We said a few ciaos and he was on his way to do some business. I didn't ask him how he'd gotten into the loft. It was probably better I didn't know.

There were lots of things I didn't know, I was soon to discover. The following evening, just as I was leaving the loft to catch Willie's last night at Radio City, I picked up the blower to find Detective Sergeant Mort Cooperman on the other end of it.

"Upfield's the man, Tex. We've got him dead to rights and we plan to throw the whole Manhattan phone directory at him including the Yellow Pages. I hate to say it, but you done good."

"Thanks. I'll tell Willie. I'm heading down to the show now."

"There might be a slight problem with that," said Cooperman. "We tried to contact him ourselves but his people couldn't find him."

"He'll be there at showtime."

" 'Fraid not, Tex. The show's been canceled."

"Canceled?"

"You know these country singers, Tex."

"I do?"

I cradled the blower and goose-stepped over to the bottle of Jameson, from which I poured a hearty shot into the old bull's horn and made a brief toast to those few brave, not to say foolhardy, individuals who wanted to be musicians when they grew up and had attempted to do both. I killed the shot, returned to my desk, and started calling Willie's people. After a while I gave up. Nobody was home. Everybody was probably out looking for Willie. Either that or they'd all hung themselves from shower rods.

The very next morning a FedEx package arrived containing a wrapped parcel on top of which was a brief scribbled note. The note read as follows:

> "Dear Kinky,
>   Let's see how good a private dick you really are. I'm going to a hospital where there are only two directions. I will play golf on an eternal course where the caddie never tires or complains. I'm going where I can see the light. It's been fun.
>
>   Love,
>   Willie
>
> P.S. Thanks for taking time out of your busy schedule to honor my bus with your esteemed presence. May the breath of Allah blow out your ass."

I opened the parcel and found one long thick braid of red hair. I didn't need a neutron microscope to know that it had once hung from the head that had written "Turn Out the Lights, the Party's Over." Indeed, it seemed that it finally was.

"We've solved one mystery it seems," I said to the cat, "only to be confronted with yet another. We've found Upfield only to lose Willie."

The cat, of course, said nothing. To be quite honest, she'd never been a Willie Nelson fan. In fact, country music in general never failed to send her up the wall. Nor had she ever demonstrated any affinity for authority figures, particularly crooked Arizona state troopers. Indeed, it must be admitted that the cat truly did not like or trust people. She was not a people person. Very possibly, that was why we'd gotten along so well together.

I was still poring over the note, pouring Jameson, and running my fingers through Willie Nelson's hair when I heard a familiar series of war whoops emanating from somewhere in the street below. I navigated over to the window in time to see Robby and Benito performing some kind of tribal dance on the sidewalk to the amusement and/or irritation of the passersby, Robby and Benito obviously not caring which. Only the cat seemed to be looking on with any sense of cultural enlightenment in her eyes.

"Cats are Indians; dogs are cowboys," I reminded her, as I flipped the puppet head out the window to Robby and Benito. The cat, of course, did not respond.

Moments later, with the puppet head back on the top of the refrigerator, Robby proudly presented me with the medicine bundle.

"The tribal elders want you to bring this bundle to Willie," he said. "It is given with its original intent—peace, hope, and brotherly love—to the man they believe may be this generation's Bluejacket. But it is also a high honor to be the one designated as messenger to bring this special bundle to its destination. To our people, the messenger is always sacred."

"It's a nice thought, boys," I said. "But it may be a little difficult to pull off just at the moment. Willie's disappeared."

I showed Robby and Benito the note and the braid of hair and as they examined the items, I thought of the other time Willie had pulled a vanishing act. To my knowledge, no one knew to this day where he'd gone. Of course, that time he hadn't left any clues for me to find out how good a private dick I really was.

"The braid's an old Indian gag," said Benito. "If somebody fell asleep around the campfire, to be funny somebody else might come along and cut off one of his braids while he was sleeping. Possibly Willie knew about this custom."

"Possibly," I said.

"But this note," said Robby, "is not so funny. I hate to say it, but it sounds a hell of a lot like a suicide note."

I didn't disagree with Robby. In fact, the more firewater I poured down my neck, the less I was inclined to disagree with anybody. After all, I'd solved the mystery, found Upfield, successfully wrapped up the investigation, and turned the culprit over to the cops. Now all I had to do was find my goddamn client.

As the afternoon and evening wore on, Robby and Benito, who evidently weren't staying at the Plaza on this occasion, made themselves at home in the loft. This didn't bother the cat, who very possibly was looking forward to another stimulating smudging experience. It didn't bother me either. I was busy calling Willie's people, drinking firewater, and studying Willie's note, none of which seemed to be getting me anywhere fast. For their parts, Robby crashed out on the couch and Benito retired to the rocking chair with headphones on and the cat in his lap. For my part, I continued trying to see how good a private dick I was.

Around about Cinderella time, Robby and Benito snuck out on me, which wasn't terribly hard to do, since I was apparently performing a fair impersonation of a man in a coma with his head on a desk, clutching in his hand a long braid of red hair. When I came to, the cat was sleeping alone in the rocker and the boys were gone. I took a Simon Bolivar Cuban cigar out of Sherlock's head and went through the pre-ignition proceedings. Simon Bolivar, I thought, the greatest leader and lover of freedom South

America had ever known, exiled from the country they'd named after him. The human race was sick, that was all. We all needed to go to a hospital where there were only two directions. I remembered something Bolivar had once said when he'd realized his hopes for the glorious revolution had failed. When he felt for certain that his work and his life had been all to no avail. "We have plowed the ocean," he'd said.

"We have plowed the ocean," I said, sometime later, as Robby and Benito barged back into the loft, Robby with an attractive blond woman on his arm, seemingly very taken with his ample ethnic charm. "We have plowed the *ocean*," I repeated, but nobody seemed to hear me. Benito was back in the rocker with his headphones on and the cat was back sleeping in his lap. Robby and the girl had turned off most of the lights and were getting acquainted on the couch.

A short while later the unmistakable sounds, sights, and smells of intense sexual intercourse began drifting through the loft. Benito, still wearing headphones, the cat, who was now wide awake on his lap, and myself, now wide awake at my desk, all worked through the initial period of mild embarrassment and began to enjoy our designated roles as voyeurs. The intensity of the performance, including the audio portion, continued to increase until we the audience were certain that the climax could only be seconds away.

Then it happened. And as it happened, the girl turned her head and seemed to be seeing her audience for the first time. As she climaxed, a look of pure radiance and joy came across her face.

"God!" she said. "Just like *Dances with Wolves*."

Benito started laughing. Then I started laughing. Then Robby started laughing, which, if you've ever tried it, is a very difficult thing to do when you're experiencing a sexual climax.

I couldn't stop laughing, so I just folded Willie's note and put it in my pocket. I didn't need to read it again anyway. I'd already figured it out.

CHAPTER FORTY-SEVEN

Less than twelve hours later it felt like a bloody mary morning, so I was sipping one aboard the Gulfstream V as we soared almost soundlessly over the glittering Pacific. The private jet could carry thirteen passengers, but on this occasion it was carrying only two—myself and my friend John McCall, the Shampoo King from Dripping Springs. Texas, that is. There were two pilots but no flight attendants, so I had to help myself to several additional bloody marys.

John McCall was just about the only guy I knew who had the time and the money to do anything he wanted and was whimsical and trusting enough to indulge me in something as crazy as trying to locate one deliberately reclusive Willie Nelson, who, I believed, was tucked away somewhere on one of seven Hawaiian Islands. If I was really as good a private dick as I thought I was.

McCall was the head of a major mega–beauty supply empire called Armstrong-McCall, stretching from Texas to eight other states and Mexico. None of John's thousands of employees and no one I knew had ever met or seen Armstrong. John himself had always been reticent to discuss his partner if, indeed, he existed at all. Possibly the date on his carton had expired or he was hanging out with Willie Nelson. If I was wrong, and Willie's note truly was a suicide note, Armstrong could've stepped on a rainbow and still be hanging out with Willie Nelson. As Tom T.

Hall once wrote: "It could be the good Lord likes a little pickin', too." I loved all of Tom T. Hall's songs and both of his melodies.

I felt comfortable discussing the details of the Upfield case and the subsequent ongoing search for my client with John McCall. He'd been through hell a couple of times himself and come out laughing at the devil. In 1986, his entire company went belly-up, but John had brought it back bigger than ever. In 1990, McCall himself had gone belly-up. Diagnosed with deadly lymphoma cancer and with the medical experts pointing the bone at him, he'd been given only weeks to live. Yet incredibly, the cancer had turned to water and disappeared during a dream John had had aboard a plane. The doctors had never seen anything like it, but of course, that's always what they say. Either that or you'll never walk again.

"How can you be so sure he's in Hawaii?" John said now, as the silver plane flew ever westward.

"I can't be sure," I said. "But Willie loves Hawaii and thinks of it as sort of a healing place. You could say a hospital. He has a home in Maui, of course, but we won't start there. It doesn't fit his note. If I understand it correctly."

" 'Going to a hospital where there are only two directions,' " read John from the document in question.

"That was the first real tip-off. The *kama'aina,* or native Hawaiians, regularly use only two directions: *mauka,* which is toward the mountains, and *makai,* which is toward the sea."

"But if it *is* a suicide note," said McCall, "there'd also be two directions: heaven or hell."

"That's the other possibility," I said.

We travelled in silence for a while. I thought of the last time John and I had flown this far in a private jet. We'd chartered it three years ago in Australia, where we'd

toured the width and breadth of that great country in the
company of a former love of mine who was Miss Texas
1987. Of course, as my pal Don Imus likes to point out, I
was Miss Texas 1967. As well as being a world-class beauty,
Rita Jo could give the best impersonation of a kookaburra
I'd ever heard in my life. In fact, I thought I heard that
kookaburra laughing at me right now. Or could it have just
been Willie Nelson? Was he even in Hawaii at all? Was I
as good a private dick as I was cracked up to be? Was my
dick too big to box with God?

It wasn't going to be easy once we got there, I reflected, as I looked down at the ocean through an un-
cloudy day. I didn't have the Village Irregulars to help me
find Willie and I wasn't even very sure anymore, if the
truth be known, whether or not he was there at all. I had
only three old friends I could count on in Hawaii and two
of them at the moment seemed about as hard to locate as
Willie Nelson. One was John Mapes, my old Peace Corps
buddy from Borneo, the first white man I ever saw wear
a sarong, who now worked for the state of Hawaii as a
high-ranking economist and spent every other waking
hour in his kayak; another was Raven a/k/a Jeff Bloom,
whom I'd met years ago when he'd worked for Bob Dylan
and who now was a computer expert who spent every
other waking hour growing every kind of tropical plant
and orchid that exists in the universe. The third guy, and
the only one I'd been able to run down thus far, was Willis
Hoover, former columnist for the *Des Moines Register,*
former Nashville songwriter, former beekeeper, in fact just
about former everything but Miss Texas, who now was a
highly respected journalist with the *Honolulu Advertiser.*
Almost everyone I knew these days was highly successful,
highly ranked, or highly respected, it seemed. That was
one of the main reasons I preferred to work alone. Of
course, I also had Father Damien on my team in Hawaii,

but he'd been neither highly ranked, highly successful, nor highly respected in his day and besides, he'd already done all he could. Now it was up to the Kinkster. Every saint has a past, they say, and every sinner has a future.

"I've left a message for my friend Hoover in Honolulu," I said, "telling him what I needed. I've got to call him as soon as we get there."

"Call him now," said John casually. "It's only about ninety-five dollars a minute, but who's counting?"

Within moments, I had Hoover on the phone. It was still in the early dawn hours in Hawaii and he was not overly pleased to be hearing from anybody. I liked people who were grumpy when they got up, so it didn't much bother the Kinkster. Hoover, however, had done his homework.

"Jesus Christ," he said. "What time is it?"

"Time to talk about lighthouses," I said.

"Kinkyhead, this is crazy, but just maybe, it's *not* so crazy."

"That's what I'm hoping."

Indeed, I was. For Willie's fateful sentence—"I'm going where I can see the light"—could just as easily be a reference to the old Hank Williams song "I Saw the Light." Hank had often ended his shows with the song, and Willie, following in his footsteps, had often ended his shows that way. Better for him to end his shows that way than end his life that way, I thought. But, somehow, I didn't lamp Willie for a suicide. He was smart enough to take his own life, I figured. But he was just a little too crazy.

"There are twenty lighthouses on the Hawaiian Islands," Hoover intoned, apparently reading from his notes, "and all of them seem to be shining in my eyeballs at this moment. There are eight on the Big Island, two on Maui, one on Molokai, four on Kauai, and five on Oahu, where there are also thirty-four golf courses, many of which are Japanese country clubs that cost over a million dollars a year to join. I've renewed my memberships to twenty-eight of them, I believe."

"Hoover," I said, "you're an angel."

"I know," he said, "but I'm flyin' too close to the ground."

"You're in good company," I said. "Stay in touch. I'm afraid we may need additional help from you."

"What do I have to do?" said Hoover. "Blow Jim Nabors?"

The next call I made was to John Mapes, my Peace Corps pal, who, it emerged, was even less of a good sport than Hoover. I had to bear with his abuse, however, because he had circumnavigated practically every mile of shoreline on the islands. The way I saw it, Mapes was essential to this little search-and-recovery operation. Now if I could just make him see his own importance.

"What the fuck are you *doing*, Friedman?" he said, in a tone of some irritation. "Do you have any idea what fucking *time* it is?"

"Time to talk about kayaking," I said.

I ran up a fair bit of John McCall's money trying to settle Mapes down, but eventually his attitude and outlook became a trifle less agitato. It didn't take him long to grasp the gravity of the situation, but I still suspect if the subject matter had been anything other than kayaking the conversation might never have taken place.

"Yes, Friedman, I know where there's some strange, flukish water conditions on the islands. One of the places is in my house. The plumbing hasn't been working for several days. In fact, I was hoping you were the plumber."

"John, this is serious business. We've got to find the freakish currents that I described combined with a fairly deserted beach combined with a lighthouse in close prox-

imity. I want you to call Hoover for the lighthouse loca-
tions when we hang up."

"Which is right now," he said, and true to his word,
he did.

I wasn't sure if Mapes was calling Hoover, calling the
plumber, or calling the mental hospital to pick me up at
the airport, but I could only hope that he and Hoover
would get their heads together and pinpoint for me what
I prayed would be the current locus of the world's most
famous, most hard-to-find gypsy songman. Then all I had
to do was go find him, whisper a few words of wisdom,
and bring him back to the same shitty world currently
occupied by all the rest of us.

But did Willie Nelson really want to be found? I had
to assume that he did or he wouldn't have sent me the
note and the braid of hair. Unless, of course, he'd underes-
timated my powers of detection and figured I'd never find
him. But what else could the braid and the note have
signified? That he was tired of the responsibility of being
a living legend? That he was taking a little sabbatical for
the rest of his life? That one more chorus of "Mamas
Don't Let Your Babies Grow Up to Be Assholes" might
send him into a hideous rictus of projectile vomiting, possibly even squirtin' out of both ends? Sometimes the road
can be enough to send you over the edge. Out where the
buses don't run. Even the Honeysuckle Rose.

On the other hand, as Bob Dylan had once told me:
"When you die they let you off the hook."

I spent the remainder of the flight poring over maps
of lighthouses, beaches, tides, and currents, and talking
idly with John McCall about the scratch-'n'-sniff saddle
he'd bought that had once belonged to Jackie O., the
Rolls-Royce he'd owned that had appeared in the Beatles
movie *Help!*, and what hotels he was planning to buy in
Hawaii and New York. Small talk, actually, for a man

who'd cheated death. Material things meant little to me. For his own reasons, I knew, they meant nothing to John. The only two people who cared less about the riches of the world than John and myself were Willie Nelson, who was missing in action, and Father Damien, who'd been dead for over a hundred years and still hadn't bothered to check his portfolio. My reflections were interrupted, unfortunately, by the specially built alarm on McCall's 1919 Rolex, which informed us that the Gulfstream V would soon be landing in Honolulu. Maybe McCall hadn't cheated the devil, I thought, but he'd certainly christianed him down.

It was early in the morning when we arrived at the airport and I was somewhat surprised to see not only Hoover, but Mapes and Raven as well, all of whom were bearing multicolored leis, the flowers of which, I later learned, had been grown by Raven himself. In what seemed to me to be a mildly homosexual ceremony, they proceeded to place the leis around the necks of McCall and myself.

"Aloha," they all said.

"Of course," added Hoover, "that's the way they greeted Captain Cook, the first white man to visit the islands in 1778. He was hailed as a god."

"I was the first white man to buy a factory in Belize," said McCall. "I was hailed as a rich Texas asshole."

"Of course," said Hoover, "Captain Cook came back on Valentine's Day of the following year but nobody said 'Aloha.' "

"What'd they say?" asked McCall.

"They didn't say dick. They just killed him and ate him."

"God is good," said Mapes.

PART SIX

LOST

CHAPTER FORTY-EIGHT

LIFE'S A BEACH, they say, and who knows, they just might be right. They've never been right yet, but we all live in hope. Anyway, that's where I found him.

It was two nights later on a little secluded sand spit on the north shore of Kauai. It was a bit to the west of the Kilauea Lighthouse, which is pronounced kill-a-way'-a and it almost killed-a-kink'-stah to get there. He was standing alone on the beach in the moonlight with only his faithful golf club to keep him company. As I got a little closer I observed that he was driving the golf balls far out into the sea and reciting some kind of mantra to himself. Possibly in the spirit of Moses or perhaps Henry David Thoreau, he was talking with his God or communing with the great eternal forces of nature. As I moved still closer, I realized I'd been wrong in this assumption as I heard clearly for the first time the words he was saying.

"Shit," he said. "Sliced that son of a bitch again."

Sporting a buzz-cut haircut and naked except for a pair of biblical boxer shorts, he looked for all the world like an old wooden cross between Mahatma Gandhi and a missing child on a milk carton. When he saw me his face lit up with a smile and his eyes twinkled and all of the years and tears fell away. He seemed pleased but not surprised.

"You're a hell of a private dick, Big Dick," he said.

"You're a hell of a living legend, Willie," I said. "And we aim to keep it that way."

I told him about the resolution of the Arthur Upfield situation and he nodded, took it in stride, then hit another golf ball halfway to Maui. We both watched as it arced over the waves, gently, inaudibly splashing down like a little whitecap on the moonlit horizon. I gave him the medicine bundle, told him the legend of Bluejacket, told him how highly the Indians held him in regard.

"They think of you," I said, "as the modern-day Bluejacket who may yet bring harmony and understanding."

He gently placed the medicine bundle on the sand next to him, teeing up another ball in the same motion. Then he hooked a ball in the general direction of Waikiki Beach.

"Shit," he said. Then as an afterthought: "Tell 'em I'm sorry so many of 'em had to die in all those John Wayne movies. His horse was *never* very smart."

"Are you ever coming back, Willie?" I said.

"Let me answer your question like this," he said, taking a joint about the size of a surfboard from behind his ear and placing it in his mouth. "Got a light?"

I lit the joint with a purple Bic with a hula dancer on it. She'd been in the family about forty-eight hours and we were just starting to warm up to each other. Willie inhaled deeply and his smile grew even wider and his eyes twinkled even more brightly. He passed the joint over to me and I took a few dutiful drags and passed it back to him. He inhaled deeply again, letting the smoke out so slowly that it seemed to vanish like moonbeams in the perfumed air of the islands.

"Well, Willie," I said, finally. "Are you?"

"Am I what?"

"Ever coming back."

"Just watch," he said, winking at me like a child showing off a magic trick.

And, indeed, it was.

As we stood there, somewhere in the neighborhood of two hundred golf balls came wading up onto the sand, pushed along by the tide like little baby ducklings. By the time they came to a stop they were all in a row at our feet. Willie just leaned on his driver and watched them coming in, proud as any mother duck.

"There's some kind of a freak rip current out there," he said, gazing out at the moon-streaked sea. "Found it by accident, except there are no accidents. Brings the balls back in about every two hours almost like clockwork."

"Jesus Christ."

"Hasn't brought Him back yet. But to answer your question, if those golf balls can keep comin' back, I probably will, too."

"That's great to hear."

"But not in two hours," he said. "Maybe in two years. Want to hit a few?"

"No, thanks," I said. "The last two good balls I hit was when I stepped on the garden rake."

"Maybe your stance was too wide," he said.

Later, we took a short walk together, for it was a very small beach. That was the way I would remember him. A little gingerbread man under the storybook stars. Born to poverty, rich in the coin of the spirit. Fragile and strong, ephemeral and timeless, beautiful beyond words and music. His guitar was not, like the great Woody Guthrie's, "a machine that killed fascists." Rather it was a machine that helped heal the broken hearts of other people and sometimes, just maybe, his own as well.

As we walked together along the sand I could see the palm trees sway and the warm Pacific Ocean embrace the nighttime shoreline of the world in Willie's eyes. I waited in near-religious silence under the cathedral of the sky for the last living folk hero in America to impart any message to his fans, friends, and family on the mainland. Yet he did not say a word until I finally ended the silence by rapidly expelling a rather large amount of gas. Then, at last, he spoke.

"I'm glad we're not on the bus," he said.

"Willie," I said, "what does God think of you out here doing nothing but smoking a joint and hitting golfballs into the sea?"

"Oh, She doesn't mind," he said. "She's always guided all my actions. Sometimes I can almost feel Her big, black hand on my shoulder as She whispers in my ear."

"What does She whisper?"

" 'Fuck 'em if they can't take a joke.' "

Then he picked up his driver, teed up a ball, and, with the joint still clamped firmly between his jaws, took another mighty swing. This one sailed straight and true over the perfect, silver ocean and seemed to go on forever.

ACKNOWLEDGMENTS

I'M WRITING THIS on a yellow legal pad of the kind favored by Richard Nixon, in longhand, stark naked in the standing position, in the fashion of Ernest Hemingway. We don't know how Hemingway hosed, but this is how he wrote. If you try it yourself you'll soon understand not only why Nixon resigned from the presidency but also why, as Charles Bukowski once put it, "ol' Hem blew his brains into the orange juice one morning."

When you write in this manner you seek, quite naturally, an economy of words as well as, of course, an economy of nerds. That's why I've chosen a small, very secluded hotel on the southeast coast of Australia accessible only by water. There's no one like Ratso around to tempt you with: "Hey, Kinkstah! Let's go to Big Wong's, baby!" There's no one like my friend Captain Midnite to enter a crowded room and shout to you in stentorian tones: "Is it wrong for a man to love another man?" No kids. No pool. No pets. Just Roger Miller's eternal soul reincarnated as a nearby kookaburra, encouraging you to wind up your latest book or song or incarnation.

Earlier this afternoon, while taking a break from the rather tedious chore of graciously thanking other people, I was having sexual relations with a young Australian bird not related to the kookaburra. You're only as young as the woman you feel, they say, and I felt like I was right back in the womb until I heard a still, small voice in my hotel room and realized it wasn't my conscience.

"Hi," it said. "I'm here to check the minibar."

"I'm right in the middle of someone," I said.

"If this is a bad time, Mr. Friedman—"

"What makes you think this is a bad time?" I said. The girl was shivering beneath me under the covers in a rictus of terror. "God wouldn't have created minibars," I continued, "if He hadn't intended for man to check them."

"Well, I'm glad you feel that way, Mr. Friedman. You just go about your business and I'll be through in a minute."

"So will I," I said.

"Wow," said the guy, now entirely focused on his work, "you must've had quite a party last night."

"I was here alone," I said. "But, of course, I'm not now."

"I've seen some strange things in this old hotel," the guy continued, oblivious. "There was Oscar Wilde bending over a new page. There was an old guy with long white hair playing the violin while getting a blow job from Marilyn Monroe. Had his old bicycle parked in the hallway, for Christ's sake. There was a guy named Seymour Glass with a hole in his head. Barely touched the minibar. Couldn't tell if Glass was half full or half empty. Get it?"

"That's a cute one," I said, chuckling along good-naturedly while I waited for the guy to stock the minibar. I wasn't really in a position to argue.

"What's this paper on the floor, Mr. Friedman? It looks important."

"Read it," I said. "Let's see how it scans." The girl now was making little hysterical gulping noises that indeed did seem to sound somewhat similar to the kookaburra.

" 'I want to thank all my teachers, rabbis, and dope-dealers for helping me get where I am,' " he read.

"Keep going," I said.

" 'I want to thank my agent Esther Newberg, who's been with me twelve years; my editor, Chuck Adams, who's been with me six years; my friend Don Imus, who's been with me twenty-four years; and the President of the United States for his encouragement and his continuing efforts to get my books made into a movie.' Can I ask you a question?"

"Spit it," I said, starting to run out of charm.

"Do you really know Don Imus?"

"Keep going," I said.

" 'The author would also like to thank Tom Friedman, Piers Akerman, Marcie Friedman, Steve Rambam, Max Swafford, and Dr. Jay Wise for their help with the manuscript; Carolyn Reidy at Simon & Schuster; Joann Di Gennaro and Erin Marut at Simon & Schuster Publicity; Jack Horner in Esther Newberg's office; Cheryl Weinstein in Chuck Adams's office; and Ted Landry, production editor. The book couldn't have been the important social document that it is without the cooperation and inspiration provided by Willie Nelson and his entire extended gypsy family. This includes David Anderson, Willie's personal assistant, for his political, spiritual, and sexual guidance throughout the author's journey.' "

"Keep going," I said.

" 'Finally, my thanks to Judith D. Allison, who knew I was writing a mystery about Willie Nelson, came up with the title *Roadkill*, and called it in from the Ritz Hotel in Paris to my mangerlike, mucus-colored trailer somewhere in the Texas Hill Country.' "

"Are you through with the minibar?" I asked. The young girl beneath me was now breathing somewhat erratically, possibly the unfortunate victim of an asthma attack.

"Sure, Mr. Friedman, but the ending to these acknowledgments sounds a bit stiff to me."

"Something has to be stiff around here," I said.

The guy was walking away from the minibar with such an aura of unfulfillment about him that I felt I had to come up with a zippier closing argument. By this time, indeed, my relationship with him had taken on something like the proportions of Captain Ahab's spiritual involvement with Moby Dick, not to mention my own.

"Okay," I said. "I was walking through Nike Village at the Olympics one day and I saw a guy with a long stick on his shoulder. So I asked him: 'Are you a pole-vaulter?' 'No, I'm German,' he said. 'But how did you know my name?' "

"Much better," said the guy, chortling to himself like an outpatient as he left the room.

The young girl's body seemed very tense beneath me. I didn't know if she was dead or merely wished that she were.

"Are you all right?" I asked.

"Keep going," she said.

ABOUT THE AUTHOR

© JODY RHODEN

KINKY FRIEDMAN lives in a little green trailer in a little green valley deep in the heart of Texas. There are about ten million imaginary horses in the valley and quite often they gallop around Kinky's trailer, encircling the author in a terrible, ever-tightening carousel of death. Even as the hooves are pounding around him in the darkest night, one can hear, almost in counterpoint, the frail, consumptive, ascetic novelist tip-tip-tapping away on the last typewriter in Texas. In such fashion he has turned out ten novels including *The Love Song of J. Edgar Hoover, God Bless John Wayne, Armadillos & Old Lace*, and *Elvis, Jesus & Coca-Cola*. Two cats, Dr. Scat and Lady Argyle; a pet armadillo called Dilly; and a small black dog named Mr. Magoo can sometimes be found sleeping with Kinky in his narrow, monastic, Father Damien–like bed.

I ONLY HOPED that if I had to go puppet headless for a while it wouldn't threaten my growing success as a private investigator. The past few years particularly, while certainly not a major financial pleasure for the Kinkster, had at least established my reputation in the city as a canny, crepuscular, cat-loving crimesolver. I'd found a few cats and a few people and a few skeletons in the closet and now I was trying to find a way not to turn into a skeleton myself, because none of my last three cases had brought in any bucks. My erstwhile Dr. Watson, Larry "Ratso" Sloman, still waiting to inherit slightly under fifty-seven million dollars from his birth mother's estate, which I helped him locate, had steadfastly kept me still waiting to inherit his bill. Likewise, in a case my reporter friend Mike McGovern had dubbed "The Love Song of J. Edgar Hoover," a chain of cowboy logic had led Stephanie Du-Pont and myself to Florida where we almost discovered Al Capone's long-lusted-after buried treasure. But the deeper we dug the shallower became our trust in each other, until at last we'd managed to bury what was left of our friendship in a similarly shallow grave.

In the brokenhearted, dispirited down time that followed Florida, my PI pal Rambam and I rounded up the

culprit in a fairly murderous little matter surrounding
America's last living folk hero, Willie Nelson. Subse-
quently, I was able to locate the reclusive redhead who
himself had gone into hiding for reasons that I cannot
divulge in this family newspaper. Nelson did not especially
appreciate being found and, though he's back on the road
again, the two of us, while remaining spiritually close, have
maintained a somewhat lesser degree of social intercourse
and certainly no sexual intercourse. Indeed, I haven't been
involved in sexual intercourse with anyone for quite a
while now and I hate to think of all that hummingbird
semen going to waste. If the truth be told, because of a
rather fortunate gene pool, I have a large penis like Ernest
Hemingway, not a small penis like F. Scott Fitzgerald.
Now the only matter I still have to resolve is whether I
want to blow my fucking brains out or merely drink myself
to death.

So, the net result of several years of difficult and
daunting detective work has been that Ratso's hardly
speaking to me, Willie's barely singing to me, and my
rather rocky, acerbic relationship with Stephanie has gone
from a romantic, quixotic dream to a tedious, ubiquitous
nightmare. The field of amateur detective work, however,
is often fallow, often fraught with frightfully forbidden
fruit from which the detective himself often reaps a har-
vest of hatred. This is because everyone says they want the
truth, but once the truth is known, few, if any, want to deal
with it. Sometimes not even the investigator himself. A
couple more successes like the ones I'd recently had, I
figured, and the cat and I would be about ready for a
time-share arrangement in Van Gogh's old padded cell.

Such were my deep, metaphysical thoughts as Sunday
morning scuttled along into Sunday afternoon much in the
manner of a wayward, oblivious dung beetle. I was smoking another cigar, drinking another shot of Jameson's, and

watching the black and white football players tump over on my old black and white television set when the lesbian dance class kicked into high gear overhead and the two red telephones on opposite sides of the desk sprang to life at the same time. This was not surprising, really, because they were both connected to the same line. It was also not surprising to see the cat do a double back flip because she was sleeping precisely midway between the two phones.

"My my," I said, "suddenly the loft has become an Africanized beehive of activity."

The cat, of course, said nothing. She sat on the desk and licked lazily at her paw, pretending the embarrassing incident hadn't happened at all. The ability to laugh at one's self is noticeably absent in virtually all cats and also in the vast majority of adult human beings. In human beings, we call this condition by its clinical name: late-blooming serious. In cats, of course, it is not a condition at all; it is merely the way of their people.

I took a few peaceful puffs on the cigar to settle my nerves and then picked up the blower on the left.

"Start talkin'," I said.

"Hummingbird dick."

"Ah, my frail little five-foot-eleven Aryan flower. So nice of you to call now that you're back in the city."

"I've lost my key to the building, Hebe. Otherwise, I would've—Pyramus! Thisbe! Stop chewing on that puppet head—"

"What?"

"Relax, nerd. I've taken it away from them."

"Well, drop it off sometime on your way down. By the way, sorry things didn't work out for you in Florida."

"What makes you think things didn't work out, fuck-brain?"

"Well, I mean, you came back—"

"So did John Travolta, but of course, he owes it all

to Scientology. And I don't recall him bringing you any bucks."

"Bucks?"

"No, not the little deer with the little antlers that you big, brave Texans blow away every year—"

"Not *all* Texans—"

"I'm talkin' cash, dickhead. Your share of the cash. A deal's a deal. I'm a girl who keeps her word."

"Well—"

"What's the matter with you? Are you brain dead? This is the part where you're supposed to say 'How much?' "

"Okay. How much?"

"Your take is seven."

"Seven dollars doesn't go as far as it used to."

"Try seven *million* dollars."